To Ashley —
my favorite ASU
student —

Seafood Jesus

Best wishes.

Julie

a novel by
Julie E. Townsend

MINT HILL BOOKS
MAIN STREET RAG PUBLISHING COMPANY
CHARLOTTE, NORTH CAROLINA

Cover art courtesy of iStockphoto.com

The author would like to express her thanks to friends who helped along the way and then some: Dr. Denise Vultee, Dr. Fred Vultee, Diane Suchetka, Karen Camburn, Dr. Glenn Hutchinson, and Craig Renfroe.

Library of Congress Control Number: 2010940396

ISBN: 978-1-59948-280-4

Produced in the United States of America

Mint Hill Books
Main Street Rag Publishing Company
PO Box 690100
Charlotte, NC 28227-7001
www.MainStreetRag.com

The world that jibes your tenderness
Jails your lust.
Bewildered by the paradox of all your musts.

—Carson McCullers

I WAS NOT RETARDED

I've been inside my head for so long, long, that it's become my cocoon, only I, I never get to emerge as a butterfly. I know what it's like to be dead, be dead, while the rest of the world lives. This thing, called "my body" by most, and "temple" by those who know the distinction, has been useless to me for longer than I can remember, can remember. Even inside this shell, this shell, I am aware of when the lines cross, lines cross, like when I think I'm past a thought, and it echoes inside. I see them when they bathe me, feed me, and clean my messes, but I feel nothing of the physical. Emotions are the only thing I still feel, still feel, but can no longer show. I can't get my body to tell my story. It can't scream, smile, or cry. If I could get it to, I would, I would. My lips would move and tell about a large, famous family, and the "me" I used to be. How many times I was reminded of how different I was, was. More different than I am now, am now. My first echo told me I was not like them. I listened to that echo in the morning and sometimes into the night. Sometimes, I was so busy following this echo that I forgot where I was, was.

Father didn't. In his business of us, he mapped, he mapped out our entire lives on a piece of paper—a report card, card of our lives. Joe Junior made the honor roll every year since birth; Jack, almost straight A's.

I always flunked, always flunked.

Father had his reasons; I had mine.

It angered him when the world interrupted his plans, plans: Joe Junior's plane exploded. Jack would have to be president, president.

Father sent me away for a lobotomy, lobotomy.

Before I left home that morning, he spoke with me in his office; his special office: the one that had a direct line to Wall Street to Chicago and to the White House, White House. I decided not to plead anymore. He thought an operation was going to make me forget, make sure that I was never an embarrassment again. Not that I ever did anything to embarrass him, him. Only when the press heard that something was wrong with me did he consider his usual measures. I have always wondered why he was so scared; why he amassed such a fortress fortune, fortune. Against what?

Maybe Eunice and I should not have gone, gone to Switzerland that summer. Maybe then I would not, would not have found the answers to my mystery.

After he found out, we wrote cryptic, cryptic ads in *The New York Times*. My favorite ad was unfortunately the last, read, "Boston's Harbor brims full of hate. Swim before it's too late."

We were supposed to meet at Old South Meeting Hall, Hall. Somehow father figured it out, out.

I rebelled. I pretended not to be able to do anything. Father knew. But father told the rest of the family that something was wrong with me, me. Yes, something was wrong with me—him!

He built his case against me swiftly, swiftly, and then convicted me before I had a chance to tell anyone why he put me on a train, even Jack, even Jack.

2   Julie E. Townsend

I told him that you cannot cut, cut people out of your life with surgical scissors.

It was all so innocent anyway.

I've heard it all, in echoes, in echoes. I float in and out of years. Time has never held much credence for me. Does it change my situation or anyone's because of a date? Sometimes it's fall and we're all in Martha's Vineyard. Sometimes it's dinner at home, and someone is cutting my meat because they think I can't, I can't. I've heard them whisper "retarded." They measure me like they do time, time.

I told Jack about the echoes, and he told me not to tell father.

I wonder if bullets echo inside, inside.

He asked me once, "What echoes?" I told him my longings. I tried to tell him what makes a longing, longing.

I think now it is a whisper from a wave of my childhood, childhood, when I climbed up on our weather-beaten bench on the pier with its planks creaking and swaying to the ocean, watching Jack and his girlfriends walk past me holding hands or stretching their arms as far as they could go around each other, each other. The way they smiled; they smiled at each other. The smile caught in the faint night light; the wooden light post swaying, swaying. Whispers of my sisters bragging about the boys they kissed. I couldn't explain, couldn't explain, why I would rather be with my girlfriends than face the musk and sweat of little boys who take this scent into manhood. I longed for something else, else: dreams father couldn't buy, couldn't buy. My longing wasn't about a kiss, a kiss.

I still think about *her* a lot: just this morning, when Stek wheeled me down the ramp, ramp. I like his silky dark blue handkerchief tucked inside his white front coat pocket. Sometimes, if I work the left side of my face into a drool, drool, rolling down like the slopes we used to sled, he takes

that pretty handkerchief out of its safe place and pats my
face dry, dry.

It feels like her touch.

You never forget a woman's touch.

They are mother, sister, friend, and lover fingers.

I hear echoes, echoes.

MYRTLE BEACH

"They" say *life flashes* can occur if your car spins out of control on a thunderstorm-saturated, oil-laden highway. Maybe before the flashes begin…before you may have involuntarily pushed your own rewind button… your hands clutch the steering wheel in an ironic symbol of the cycle of life.

Maybe you don't clutch it at all as you careen into that not-so-conveniently-planted, seventy-two-year-old oak, as you hope that the last words you utter won't echo, "Sssshhhhiiiiiiiiiiiittttt!" (It's not exactly the way you want to be remembered.)

Maybe you think about random historical facts that you haven't thought about since college, like General George Custer, and why Custer's muster helped to bury his own blond curls at the Battle of Little Big Horn.

Maybe you hear what Custer did not: a flock of seagulls, flapping their wings in a solidarity of beats, in hunger of their next feeding.

Or maybe you remember the first and only time you were in love; maybe you remember how your whisper still remains a whisper.

Leslie Ryan had not wrecked her 2009 black BMW...the one that she had purchased after her last commercial real estate sale before the Great Recession really kicked in; there wasn't an oak tree in sight, but she was clutching the steering wheel with the same crash vigor as she looked at the clock on her dashboard and calculated that only thirteen minutes had passed since her mother had reminded her again what she really thought about "it." The "it" they managed like an international cold war, dancing around the issue like they were competing on *Dancing with the Stars*; the "it" that made "it" her own personal *Schindler's List*. The "it" discussion that might as well as have doubled as an oak tree wreck, because, when Leslie's mother finally divulged her role in Rosemary Kennedy's lobotomy over sixty years ago, she did it like a cat hissing just for the hell of it. But her mother didn't stop there. She watched as Leslie looked down at the white linen tablecloth, and as Leslie raised her head back up, her mother utilized the most potent of her emotional terrorist weapons: God had, in all likelihood, caused the death of Andrea, Leslie's partner of ten years.

That's why Leslie left her mother sitting at Morton's, lobster steaming under her nostrils, and why she was stuck in one of the six lanes of Highway 17 in Myrtle Beach, on a weekend summer night, with the 450,000 people who invaded it from Memorial Day to Labor Day, when buffet bars made a killing, feeding hungry families of four. Well, here they were, she thought: all 450,000 of them.

Leslie pounded on the steering wheel as she inched along with the other cars: stately Chryslers packed with stately-looking men, driving with women whose hair was either solidly white or partially blue; and Jeeps crammed with teenagers blaring their stereos, moving to the beat like they had a dance floor in the back seat.

She replayed the dinner scene in her head again—her mother's sardonic smirk when she had said, "God hates fags, and that's why Andrea had to go."

Leslie had responded by saying, "Andrea isn't, I mean, wasn't a fag, mother. And guess what? I'm not a fag either. If you're going to use derogatory language, at least get it right. I'm not a gay man!"

As Leslie thought about this conversation, she jerked her cell phone up from the passenger's seat and pushed in 4-1-1. Within seconds, she heard, "What city please?"

"Myrtle."

"Go ahead."

"I'd like a number to a gay bar."

"Excuse me?"

"I'd like a number to a gay bar."

"We don't have them divided up."

"Oh," Leslie said, and thought, *But they sure as shit have them divided up everywhere else.*

"You might want to call the local gay switchboard."

"Yes, thank you."

"Hold for the number."

Leslie punched it in as the computerized voice gave her the number.

A man with a nasal, country-southern voice answered. "The Grand Strand's Gay/Lesbian Switchboard. Can you hold please?" His "please" sounded like "pleaaaase."

He didn't wait for Leslie to answer. She wondered why people bothered asking.

"Yes," she said anyway to suspended air time. Leslie pictured him as tall, lean and mustached. She often visualized what people she had never met looked like from how they sounded. She could usually come within an inch or two of height, a shade of hair color, six months in age, the number of wrinkles, clothing style, and even the region of the state they were from.

"Thank you for holding. How may I help you?"

"I'm from out of town and was wondering if you could tell me if there are any gay bars in Myrtle."

"Where you from, sweetie?" he asked.

Friendly, Leslie thought, but maybe he was testing her. Could anyone call up and get this information? What if some psycho called and got the address?

"Charlotte."

"Have you heard the joke about Charlotte?" He began laughing without waiting for her answer, just as he had when he'd put her on hold.

"Why does Charlotte have so many gay men?" Again, he didn't wait for her answer. "Because it's the Queen City!" He snorted. She envisioned the edges of his mustache curling downward. She thought he probably dyed it.

"That's funny," she said, trying to sound jovial, but it wasn't that funny. At least he wasn't a straight person saying it for a change.

"Charlotte has some great bars. Been out to any?" He had to be testing her.

"Not in years."

"Years? Girl, it's time to twirl." He laughed again.

"The last one I went to was Scorpio."

"Old Scorpio," he said, and she thought he sounded wistful. "I remember when it had a lighted dance floor like the scene from *Saturday Night Fever*."

"I remember that," she said. That was the only time she and Andrea had gone to a gay bar for retro disco night. They couldn't stop watching a woman who had on the same kind of white polyester suit and black shirt John Travolta had worn. They were amazed at how her hair was blown up and back just like his.

"Now that's a woman who isn't afraid of flaunting her sexuality," Andrea had said.

"Flaunt?" Leslie had retorted. "She might as well go ahead and have a penis attached."

Andrea had only shaken her head. "Maybe she's risking it all for a chance to be happy."

Andrea was always more accepting of and sympathetic toward those whom Leslie considered too flamboyant...just too far over the sexual scale. Whether it was a gay man's flailing hands and high-pitched voice, or the deep voices of women who Leslie believed went to barber shops instead of salons for their mannish hair cuts, it always made her cringe...cringe because she didn't understand the extremes; cringe because she was embarrassed that her relationship made her an instant member of a social/political club she had never officially joined.

Her thoughts about Scorpio ended when the guy on the switchboard said, "I don't know what kind of bar you prefer—mostly women or mixed—but the one with the best music is The White House. It's between 66th Avenue and Magnolia Street. But it doesn't get hopping until eleven or so."

"Thanks. I appreciate the information."

"That's what we're here for, and say 'hello' to the Queen City."

She was getting ready to put her cell phone down when he added, "Have you seen that statue of Queen Charlotte on the corner of Fifth and College? Doesn't it look like Barney Fife in drag?" He started laughing again.

"Never thought about it, but I think you're right." Leslie forced a laugh. If only her mother could have his sense of humor. But she didn't want to think about her right now.

"Nice talking to you," he said, hanging up before she could thank him again.

She set the phone down on the passenger's seat just as someone blew the horn. The light was green, but no one was moving; she only had to drive a few more blocks. She glanced at the clock on the dashboard. Nine o'clock. So what if the bar wasn't "hopping" yet? She could find a table and watch all the unstable people her mother lumped her with, which meant anyone who was left of her mother's right. Or, rather, wrong of her mother's right.

It was always full circle with them.

At the third red light, she turned left and drove two blocks.

The bar was on the second floor of an old white two-story cinder-block building. She supposed that's why it was called "The White House." Maybe it was a gay joke. A staircase in the middle of the building led to the second floor, but she could see only five of the stairs; the rest of them disappeared into darkness. She saw a small blue-and-red sign, pulsating with the words "The White" in blue, "House" in red.

As she sat in her car, still clutching the wheel, she glanced around the parking lot. Four men were walking up the steps.

Maybe she shouldn't go in. Some retribution. So she and her mother got into it again for the first time in years. Was a gay bar in Myrtle Beach going to make her feel any better about that? Or solve what she was going to do about the real estate deal? The largest deal of her commercial real estate career? After her mother's divulgence about Rosemary Kennedy and her biblical claims about Andrea, the real estate deal that might go awry was the last of the night's insults. It had already pole-vaulted Leslie into an emotional overdose mode, oak tree or oil-laden highway or not. Her anger about her mother's comments made Leslie think that if she went through with the real estate deal, the Rosemary situation would feel like a piece of gravel compared with the pending boulder of her brokerage.

As Leslie still sat in her BMW, she noticed three rotund, masculine women waddling like ducks toward the entrance.

She squeezed the steering wheel hard. "I'm not like them," she said to herself. "I'm nothing like them."

When the women began walking up the stairs, Leslie got out of her car, her high heels sinking into the sandy parking lot. She slung her purse over her shoulder, her hand shaking as she tucked the keys into the side pocket. She felt like she did when she called on a client for the first time—the bipolar emotions: confident they would want to do business with her; certain they would think her incapable of selling their five-million- dollar building. But she whispered the mantra she had begun saying the day after Andrea died: "Fuck it, fuck it, fuck it."

She walked up the flight of stairs to where two men sat behind a table with a pink flamingo lamp on top of it. One of the men looked beefy in his black tank top, like he should have yards of chest hair, but he was hairless. She supposed the collage of tattoos that covered his arms made up for the lack of hair. He looked like a Hell's Angel: a gay Hell's Angel, she thought. Did they have a Chapter? The other man looked like a stockbroker: starched shirt, tie, red suspenders, and cuffed beige pants.

The stockbroker guy spoke to her.

"Got a membership?" Not waiting for her answer, he stuck a rubber stamp into an ink pad.

"I'm not from here."

He turned toward the tattooed guy. "Harry, sign her in as your guest."

Harry didn't say anything, but he leaned over and scrawled out his name in one column of some papers clipped to a board.

"Sign your name. Need to see your driver's license. There's a five-dollar cover."

Leslie leaned over to sign her name beside Harry's. She opened her purse and then her wallet. She handed the stockbroker a five-dollar bill and held her license up.

"Charlotte, huh?" The stockbroker guy asked.

She wondered why people always asked the obvious.

"The Queen City," he said to Harry. But when he said "Queen," it rolled off his tongue like he was making an announcement: "And the winner is...the Quuuuueeen City."

"Have you heard the joke about Charlotte?" Harry asked. His voice shocked her. She thought Harry, the gay Hell's Angel, would have a voice that thundered like Zeus's. Instead he sounded like one of the munchkins from *The Wizard of Oz*. If she had heard him on the phone and then seen him, her voice theory would have had its first refutation.

"Yeah, I've heard it," but she didn't look at him.

What was the deal with Charlotte? she wondered. What did people do here all day, sit around and make up Charlotte jokes?

She snapped the button on her purse and flung it back onto her shoulder.

Harry looked at the stockbroker and said it was going to be a busy night. No, she thought. Maybe he sounded more like he sucked on a helium balloon for breakfast.

Leslie walked past their table and through an open door frame to go into the actual bar. As she walked into it, she felt a jolt of nervousness, like she had just shot up five cups of coffee, extra-leaded. She stopped, acting as if she were fumbling for something in her purse, wondering whether she should turn around now and forget this secret mission against her mother. But the bartender decided it for her, his voice dividing her fear in two. For a second, she thought it was a woman with a deep voice wanting to buy her a drink. Not that there would be any. She had often thought it was a good thing she knew she was fairly attractive, because pitting her self-esteem against a bar crowd, straight or gay — a crowd that never paid her any attention — would have sent her esteem crashing like a jumbo jet. At five-foot-five, with no gray hairs or love handles yet, Leslie was the kind of pretty that grew on you. She knew this about herself. So maybe she didn't saunter into a place, walking like a model on a runway — left foot in front of right, right in front of left — but she didn't walk side-to-side like the women she saw walking into the bar a few minutes ago. Her dark brown hair was stylishly layered down her slender neck, and her tapered nails, always professionally done, emanated a glossy finish. So even if men or women didn't trip on themselves just for a chance to meet her, she knew that her green eyes would eventually be admired, as well as her taut butt. But her kind of pretty was never a match for Andrea's striking beauty. Andrea's beauty could be seen and felt even in the dark of night. She once told Andrea, "Someone had to be the ugly duckling."

"You really have missed your calling in life," Andrea had said in response to Leslie's comment. Then she had added, "You know you're pretty, and I'm not going to puff up your shallow ego tonight."

Leslie's memory was interrupted when the bartender asked, "What can I get for you, honey?"

"Chardonnay."

"Chablis all right with you?"

"That's fine."

"Wanna run a tab?" he asked as he poured her wine.

"No thanks." She scanned the bar, looking for a place to sit. She wanted to hide behind one of the fake ferns.

"Seven-fifty." He set the glass in front of her.

She opened her purse, laid a ten dollar bill on the bar, and took a sip of wine. It tasted cheap, unlike the wine she and her mother had sipped on earlier at one of the most expensive restaurants in Myrtle Beach.

"Keep the change," she said.

"Thanks, Sweetie."

She took another sip. At least it seemed to burn away some of her anxiety about walking into a gay bar. Ten years. She did an inventory of it, like she did when she assessed commercial property: a large dance floor with a lighted floor, two bars, three pool tables, DJ booth, a smattering of tall tables with barstools; one, two, three...five, six fake ferns. Class C retail space.

The DJ turned up the volume just as she finished counting the plants, as if she were in sync with him.

She eyed a table in the corner, near a fake fern, that would make a good spot for her to watch people; so she walked over, set her glass of wine on the table and climbed onto the stool. She smoothed the edges of her dress and crossed her legs.

The music went another notch louder.

"Sure gettin' hard to meet women. Reckon men have this much trouble? You with anyone?"

Leslie looked to her side.

A squat woman with short, spiked, dark hair was wearing blue jeans and a navy tee shirt, with a cigarette dangling out of the corner of her mouth. She was holding a bottle of beer by the neck, like she had been hunting all day, and it was her kill.

Leslie thought the woman's voice sounded Gomer-Pyle southern-fried, but deep, as if her parents had given her cigarettes instead of a pacifier at birth.

Before Leslie could respond, the woman said, "Mind if I sit with you a spell?"

She almost said "yes"—as in "Yes, I mind if you sit with me"—but she couldn't muster up meanness that quickly. Besides, Leslie's mother had always told her it was better to smile at the first initial contact...that was the southern way...and her mother always did so, with a whitened-toothed smile.

The woman wanting to sit with Leslie didn't have a whitened smile; she didn't even have a complete set of teeth.

Leslie used to swear to Andrea that she would go straight before she would be with a woman who was as masculine as a guy. Andrea would tell her, "What if she's just like me, only a dyke?"

"It's my birthday," the woman said, and as she did, her frown seemed to hang over her dark, formerly pink gums.

Julie E. Townsend

"In that case…," Leslie said.

The woman swaggered a couple of steps closer, swung her leg completely over the barstool like she was mounting a horse, and sat down.

"I'm Samantha, but my friends call me 'Squirrel.'" She set her beer down, then wiped her right hand on her jeans and stuck it out toward Leslie.

Squirrel shook Leslie's hand vigorously, like she was running for office.

Figures, Leslie thought: *a nickname*. That was another thing she didn't understand about gay women: their goddamn nicknames. One woman, whose name was Patricia, insisted on being called "Pete"; another preferred to be called "Cruise" over Celeste. "Cruise?" What kind of name was that? Short for Tom? A lesbian who liked to drive? A lesbian vacationing in the Pacific?

"I'm Leslie, and my friends call me 'Leslie.'" She thought that her response sounded like a scene from *Forrest Gump.*

Squirrel laughed. "Guess how old I am."

"I'd rather not."

"Think you'd hurt my feelings if you don't get it right?" Squirrel took a gulp of her beer. "I've got a theory about ages, so it don't matter nohow."

"What, that we get better with age?" Leslie asked sarcastically and then took a sip of her wine.

"Maybe I'll tell you later." Squirrel took a long swig of her beer. "So guess my age."

"Forty-three?"

"That's what I get for asking. Thirty-four. I'm thirty-four today."

"Happy Birthday."

"How old you?" When she asked this, Leslie noticed how Squirrel didn't use a verb, and how her "you" sounded more like "ewe." Definitely a southern-fried accent.

"I'm thirty-five."

"What sign are you?"

"Let's skip the horoscopes tonight."

"Okay." Squirrel looked down at her beer and turned the bottle around, then leaned her elbow on the table. "I just bet you're a Scorpio."

"No prize tonight," Leslie said, and then she took a sip of wine.

"You ain't from around here, are you?"

"How did you know that?"

"'Cause ain't nobody dresses like what you got on, 'cept the drag queens." Squirrel looked her up and down as she took another gulp of her beer.

Leslie had forgotten that she had on a black cocktail dress with high heels. She didn't know that she was going to leave her mother stranded in a fancy restaurant and end up at some podunk gay bar in Myrtle Beach, cornered by her first dyke in ten years. At least ten years ago, she could point to Andrea and say, "That's my girlfriend," and see the smile turn downward like an inverted crescent moon before the woman would walk away. She didn't have that excuse now.

She looked around the bar. Everyone was dressed in jeans, or shorts, or dress pants, but not dresses, unless she counted the guy on the dance floor who looked like Beyoncé, wig and all.

Leslie remembered the first time she had seen a man dressed like a woman. It was the same night they had watched the John Travolta woman, only this guy was stunning as a woman. Leslie had turned to Andrea and said, "Look, a real woman." Andrea had only laughed and said, "That's a man, sweetheart."

She turned to Andrea and said, "It's confusing, you know. Women who look like boys on the verge of puberty, and men who make prettier women than the women gay women are attracted to. No wonder the rest of the world doesn't understand."

Andrea moved closer toward Leslie and put her arm around her waist. "What's so confusing?"

"This," Leslie said as she pointed to the man dressed liked a woman, "and that," as she pointed to a woman who looked like a man—and a redneck one at that—with a close-cropped haircut and a rat tail hanging down her back.

"It's only confusing when you compare surfaces," Andrea had said. Then she added, "They're art. Isn't art beautiful?"

Leslie was never quite sure exactly what Andrea meant, but now when a woman such as Squirrel was vying for her attention, she wished she had understood and appreciated it.

"How come a pretty woman like you is alone on a Friday night?" Squirrel took another drag of her cigarette, and then snuffed it out in the ashtray.

Leslie turned from watching the Beyoncé man to Squirrel.

"Kind of personal, don't you think?" she said and began looking at people dancing.

"Don't mean no harm by it. Just curious, that's all. 'Sides, it's my birthday."

Leslie looked at Squirrel as she reached into her shirt pocket for another cigarette, flicked the lighter, held it to the end of the cigarette and took a drag.

Where was her "don't-approach-me-now" aura? There had to be something that kept people away, but not Squirrel, who reminded her of men who acted like they had a compulsion to conquer. Or was it freedom? The freedom and place to flex one's wants, like Andrea had said about the John Travolta woman?

"Some man dump you?" Squirrel chugged her beer, with her cigarette dangling between her two fingers.

Leslie glared at her and felt like saying something mean—she started forming a word, her mouth slightly parted, a vowel working its way from brain to tongue to lips. But instead she took a sip of her wine. She wouldn't drown her anger, tuck it away behind home's closed doors; nor would she take it out on a stranger. Not this time.

"Squirrel, I've already dealt with enough shit for one night. I'm just not interested

Squirrel turned her face to the left, took a drag, and blew the smoke out of the corner of her mouth.

"Know what? I admire a woman who gets right to the point. You always so blunt?" And she took another drag, holding the cigarette between her thumb and index finger.

"No. Let me ask you something, are you open to your friends, family, and coworkers?"

"Do I look like I got stupid written all over my country face?" And as she said this, her eyes grew wider, and she reached for her beer.

"You don't think they know about you?"

Squirrel flicked her ashes into the ashtray. "Oh, you mean 'cause I ain't all dolled up like you? Think it gives me away?"

"That and the way you swagger."

Leslie wished she hadn't said that because Squirrel's face fell fast—a smile gone south for the winter. But before she could apologize, Squirrel said, "Maybe I'm more of a dead giveaway than somebody like you" (and she still said "ewe"). "Like to think leastwise I was cute." She looked away as she took a swig of her beer, still holding the bottle by its neck.

Leslie took another sip of wine.

"Don't matter nohow. Me and you in the same net."

Leslie raised her glass as in a toast. "To being alone and on a birthday too."

"Ain't what I'm talking 'bout."

Squirrel looked around the bar. Leslie followed the direction of her head.

Leslie watched two women hugging each other in a dark corner of the bar. They kissed in the shadows of the flickering lights that moved quickly across the dance floor like clouds reflecting on a road ahead during a windy day. Leslie thought cloudscapes, kisses and darkness could evoke the most meager of sexual urges and turn them into love-lust on a moment's notice. Leslie could see that, but she would hold out for what she had with Andrea. That was the problem, though. She knew that what she had with Andrea wasn't going to come waltzing into her life. That was like winning the Powerball twice.

Squirrel looked back at Leslie. "Way I figure it, we're all in this together. Gotta watch out for each other lessen we get steamed or deep-fried like captured seafood."

Leslie gulped the rest of her wine and looked at Squirrel. "I need to get going," she said as she swung her feet to the side so she could get off the stool.

"Ain't something I said, was it?"

"It's been an experience meeting you."

"Likewise I'm sure. Maybe I'll see you out this way again sometime," she said as she took another drag off of her cigarette. This time she didn't blow to the side.

Leslie watched the smoke drift in front of her, and then turned to walk away. No, it wasn't anything Squirrel had said; it was everything she had meant to say. How they were all an unprotected, endangered species, swimming in the ocean: always prey; prey for anyone who needed an issue to win an election; prey for anyone who felt good about their hate...and how the topic of gay marriage or rights *always* came up when a national election was close. Were gay people really that stupid? Leslie wondered. Maybe, because why else would they fall prey to another election-year ploy, year after year, with false promises of the law recognizing marriage? The massive media play of countless smiling couples, emerging from their quickie "legal" gay nuptials, only to be seen again during convenient thirty-second spots of the politicians who were there to "right that moral wrong."

She clenched her jaw as she walked out to her car.

Leslie opened her car door and slammed it shut. She jammed the car keys into the ignition, and as the engine turned, she pushed the volume of the stereo up higher. She didn't care what was playing. Not this time. She would just feel the beat, let it bang between her eardrums, between the car speakers, just because; just because she was not going to go through with *the* real estate deal. A two-hundred-thousand-dollar commission, just because....

Julie E. Townsend

SEAFOOD JESUS

Valgooney Gore, a lean, naturally-tanned-year-'round, actual blond, knew she had cut it close this time— barely escaping the Coast Guard, their lights cutting through the channel's brush like a machete. Just yesterday, the Myrtle Beach Grand Strand's *Sun Times News* reported that the reward was raised to twenty-five thousand dollars. "The Crab Bandit," the article read, "has made fresh crab meat a delicacy in this area." As she cut that article out like all the others she had collected for two years, she said aloud, "Someone please tell me who our heroes are…movie stars and sports figures? A bona fide hero is one who saves lives, not a pop star who managed to make millions on some more of the same."

When the "Crab Bandit" was mentioned on the local news, the reporters speculated like all news people did, with an air of authority as thick as Myrtle Beach's humidity. "The culprit," a reporter said on the five-o'clock "first" news, "is selling the crabs and making a fortune." By five-thirty, Channel 8 claimed it had the inside story from a seafood distributor.

"Our sources tell us that these people are attempting to take over the entire market by robbing free enterprise."

She wasn't "robbing free enterprise," she thought. She was just a *seafood* Jesus. Okay, maybe the crabs wouldn't have eternal life; but at least for a while, she saved the crabs from sautéing or boiling to death. Only she never intended for her mission to get notoriety; she just didn't know how else to save them, like she had tried to do with the horses used for glue on postage stamps. For that one, she held a protest at the main post office in Myrtle Beach: posters painted with horses lying on their backs, hoofs straight up in the air; captions reading "Stop the violence," and posters of Uncle Sam pointing at his ass, with the caption "Glue this." Two hundred like-minded people showed up for that protest. Unfortunately, that anti-glue protest didn't move beyond the state line, unlike the Tea Party gatherings. Though she didn't agree with a group of people who thought they were replicating history, she at least admired how the nucleus of the movement was able to rally millions. She had given up trying to guess what exactly pissed off the sheep-following public. Instead, she didn't count a protest or movement successful unless it was capable of altering some minds. She thought that she had done so by making people aware that the stamps they slapped on envelopes used to be the race horses that they may have seen on television.

For the glue protest, she was thrown in jail for the night because she refused to leave the premises. The police charged her with "disorderly conduct."

Earl and Lola Jenkins had bailed her out that time. She was sure that wouldn't be the last time; however, she had decided then that she preferred to lurk in the shadows of the numerous causes she had instigated, funded, and seen played out in the media, like the woman who had started "pay it forward."

She wondered, though, when she was almost caught, who was more stupid: she, for almost getting caught; or the

Coast Guard, for not checking the engines along this part of the channel? Not that they could make an arrest for a hot engine, but they could have brought her in for questioning.

She knew it wasn't right to destroy others' property, but it was crueler to kill animals. Sometimes she thought it was odd that the same people who doted on their pets ate other animals and never once thought about the similarities between their cats and a little fried chicken. Just because something was a mass-production enterprise didn't mean it was void of feeling.

She probably would not have thought about destroying the underwater cages if it had not been for her hearing some vacationers describing their crab catch and then seeing some legs on display in the grocery store. The barbarianism got to her: legs being torn off of a body, any body, human or not, and then put on display for sale.

So she began zipping throughout the Intracoastal Waterway, looking for the floating plastic milk cartons that indicated a cage was directly underneath. She'd hoist the cage into her flat-bottom boat, water gushing out like a broken dam, and then she'd snap open the door of the cage. Before all of the crabs could make their escape, she'd lift it again and tilt it off the side of the boat until she heard the last plop. Then, with a surgeon's precision, she'd cut the cage apart with a pair of wire cutters and let it sink back into the water under the bobbing milk carton.

Last night she had only been able to destroy one cage before she heard the Coast Guard's boat moving slowly through a nearby channel. She saw its lights shining down the channels like they were in Vietnam on reconnaissance patrol. As she leaned over the boat and twisted the wet, dripping metal with her pliers, their rotating light shone on the end of her boat. The light stopped for a second.

She shook the cage hard and heard the crabs falling into the water. As she kept shaking the cage, she used her other hand to turn up the engine. Just as the Coast Guard's light began its counterclockwise circled scope, she tossed the cage into the marsh and sped off into the channel. She knew that their boat was too big to make it down this particular channel, but they could catch her as she came back to the main channel.

It wasn't that she feared getting caught; she just didn't want to hear what Lola Jenkins, Earl's wife, would have to say about it. When Lola was mad about something, there wasn't a planet far enough away to escape to. Valgooney closed her eyes and could see the entire drama coming in three acts. Short, squat, and sixty-five years old, Lola would first invade Valgooney's face space, standing so close to her that if either one would move a quarter of an inch, their lips would touch. Valgooney didn't care for the spittle that shot out from the corners of Lola's mouth like missiles. She could feel them land on her face—hot sprinkles—like a sharp summer drizzle. The drizzle moved to the verbal, the verbal to gesticulation, like a dictator at his own rally.

When she wanted, Lola could turn that knob within herself and burn on high for as long as it took to get her mission accomplished. Add a little righteousness to it, and it was a miracle if the person who was the focus of her anger could ever emotionally walk again. Lola, Valgooney sometimes thought, was the kind of woman who could make a man go limp with just a look, a snort, or those words that ate their own, inside out.

At least earlier tonight, Lola was on a slow simmer.

"What's that you bringin'? Goin' get me in trouble tonight," Earl said, sitting in a white rocking chair on their wide front porch.

"I thought it might sweeten Lola so she wouldn't pick on either one of us." She walked up the stone steps. "All yours." She handed him the bottle.

Earl set the bottle down, stood up and gave her a hug. "How you?"

"Fine."

Earl bent down toward the table, picked the bottle back up, and held it close to his right eye. "Gettin' fancy on us?"

"I almost didn't bring it because I wasn't sure if she was letting you get away with having a drink now and then."

Earl glanced over his shoulder toward the open front door. "Way she tell it, make somebody think I'm out cattin' around seven night a week. Ain't so. Ain't never been so, and she know it. Me havin' a drink now and then about the only thing left she can complain about." He picked up the bottle. "Fact is, I think she get downright bored when she don't have somethin' she can complain about." He looked back over his shoulder again. "Come on, let's get her goin'."

They walked through the doorway and into the wide foyer. Valgooney looked at the shiny hardwood floors. "Did you refinish these?"

"Lola made me do it last week."

They walked through another doorway and into the large kitchen. Sometimes, when Valgooney hadn't visited for a while, the size of their kitchen was shocking. Most everything was large compared with her trailer.

Valgooney did a quick 360-degree look at the kitchen: the glossy white walls and Waverly pattern melded with the hanging plants and utensils packed neatly in wooden holders.

Lola had her back to them, stirring something in one of the three tall metal pots on top of the stove.

"Lola, look what Valgooney bring," and he held up the bottle.

Lola, dressed in a light blue dress with black buttons down the front, turned around.

"How you been honey? Ain't seen you in a few weeks." They hugged.

"Told Earl you must be workin' on another project, 'cause when you do, I know you lock yourself away in that trailer and except for your runnin', you a ghost."

Not waiting for an answer, Lola walked back over to the stove. She picked up a large plastic spoon lying in the middle of the stove in a heart-shaped dish and resumed her stirring. "Cookin' you a new vegetarian dish called 'Chick Pea and Artichoke Stew.' The nurse at my doctor's office recommended it when I was havin' my blood pressure checked."

Valgooney sat down in a chair at the kitchen table. "Smells wonderful. I hope it wasn't too much trouble."

Lola kept stirring. "Don't you worry none if it was."

"What did the doctor say about your blood pressure?"

"What he always say, say it too high, but I told him I was doin' what I could without starvin' myself to death. Told him I'd never have a body like my husband. Told him God didn't intend my body to be no toothpick. I was made a pear, not a toothpick."

"Lola, you want some of this wine?" Earl had the bottle on the counter and was pulling on the corkscrew.

She nodded. "Get them nice glasses out of the china cabinet."

Earl pulled out the cork and walked into the adjoining dining room and returned with three crystal goblets. "You been readin' about the Crab Bandit? They gettin' real busy now," he said.

Valgooney didn't look at him or answer.

Earl poured the red wine into each glass. Then he picked up one of the glasses, and the wine sloshed from side to side as he walked over to Lola. "Here, Honey."

"Can't you see I'm cookin'?"

He kissed her on her cheek. "You cookin' even when you ain't." He turned and winked at Valgooney.

"Like I was sayin'," he said as he walked quickly to the table and grabbed another glass by its stem and handed it to Valgooney, "somebody been up and down the channels destroyin' crab cages extra hard. Got the Coast Guard on they butt now. Musta saved thousands of crabs bein' eaten for dinner."

"What you complainin' about?" Lola set the spoon back down on the heart-shaped dish. "Been good for business."

Earl looked at Valgooney. "People buyin' chicken necks, catchin' them the old-fashioned way. I told Lola I might have to start raisin' chickens."

He shook his head. "Somebody goin' get in some kind of trouble." He took a sip from his glass. "Goin' to get in some kind of trouble."

"Earl, why you keep sayin' that? The robber goin' pay when they catch him. Any fool know that, so shut up."

Valgooney took a sip of her wine and smiled at Earl. She knew that he knew. They had always had this connection. It was the ingredient that had made him her parents' best friend, and why he was hers. Not that she always told him everything… especially about the number of vacationers she had seduced…but even when she didn't tell him about every secret protest she was involved in, and even if it took him a while to link it to her, somehow he knew.

The first day the Crab Bandit story was on the local stations and in the regional paper, Earl knocked on her trailer door, and when she opened it, he held out the newspaper so she could see the headlines and said, "You written all over it."

"What do you mean?"

"You think you the most anonymous person this side of the ocean."

She had only laughed. The laugh stalled Earl for then, but not now, two years into it.

After dinner, they all sat out on the front porch. Lola and Earl rocked in sync in their matching chairs, while Valgooney sat on the porch and leaned against one of the wide, white pillars.

"Hear you been stirrin' up trouble again," Lola said to Valgooney.

"Told you not to bring that up." Earl said, and he stopped rocking.

"Changed my mind," and she put her foot down on the porch and stopped rocking.

"All right, but I ain't gettin' into it with you tonight, you hear?"

"Hear somethin'." Lola put her foot back up on the support slat of the chair and started rocking again.

Earl began rocking too.

"Just hope nobody goin' lose they job again. Just cause you got lots of money in the bank, don't help the maids. They don't have squat. Humph! Unionizin' maids in the South. This ain't New York, in case you ain't heard. Word out on you, girl. You the one to contact for that cause or this cause. Don't mean you gotta do it." Lola rocked her chair a little faster, like she was driving a stick-shift car and had just switched into another gear.

"Lola," Earl said.

"I don't get involved all of the time," Valgooney said.

"Humph. Name one," Lola said.

"I once turned down a group that wanted to kidnap Pat Robertson."

"Maybe that the one you shouldn't turn down. Right, Earl?"

"That right."

Earl and Lola laughed.

Valgooney didn't laugh....

William Wiley had met with her at Fullwood's Diner in Cherry Grove, and as they sat down and scooted their chairs closer to the table, he told her he had heard about the different kinds of groups she had been linked to, and that he represented a group committed to change.

"I appreciate you meeting with me, especially since I've heard that you're a recluse. May I say that you defy the stereotype of a recluse?"

Valgooney smiled at the word "recluse" as she took a sip of her coffee. How was she reclusive, when she interacted with people? What was reclusive about joining in on protests or funding countless causes? Just because she didn't have an entourage to hang out with, and just because most people bored her, and just because she didn't care whether she was with people or not…did this make her an official recluse?

Wiley said, "It wasn't easy tracking you down with the various LLC's that you have and"—he flung his hands out, palms up—"P.O. box this and P.O. box that." Then, as he reached for his coffee, he added, "It was a great surprise that you actually responded to my letter."

She took another sip and said, "You have a gift for calling attention to what torments you and your group."

"Let me elaborate on that note. Pat Robertson. He's an affront to people with an IQ in the single digits. He needs to be put out of his misery!"

Valgooney laughed and leaned back in her chair. "Okay," she said.

Wiley leaned in closer. He pursed his lips to the side as he said, "We want to kidnap him until he apologizes to the thousands of people that he has offended. If we could, we'd also get that Phelps guy too, but he's so twisted, he makes Robertson seem normal." When he finished saying this, he leaned back in his chair at the same time that Valgooney scooted hers closer to the table.

"I agree he is all that you say, and that he is probably a miserable human being. But, Mr. Wiley, he would be touted as a hero if you kidnapped him…. Is that what you want? Pat Robertson a hero? Maybe he's happy, hating. I think that you need to juxtapose."

"Juxtapose?"

"Pit the good with the bad. The bad always looks worse with juxtaposition. Work against his hate campaign, just like Dr. King did with the police in Birmingham."

"We tried, if only you knew how hard we've tried, but that son of a bitch is Teflon. He knows how to push all the bigot buttons of his constituents, and it never, never, never makes him look bad. On top of that, he always throws in the homosexuals. There's nothing more exciting than sin-making homosexuals to get Robertson smiling." Wiley slapped his hand down on the round marble table. A pinging sound accompanied the slap. As Valgooney looked down at her coffee sloshing in her cup, she noticed Wiley's gold pinkie ring.

"Sorry," Wiley said. "I just get so mad when I think we might have to endure more years of his constipated smile!"

Wiley took a sip of his coffee. Valgooney hoped it was decaf.

Wiley said, "On a lighter note, I recently heard a comedian say that Pat Robertson was a reincarnation of Pat Robertson."

"What does that mean?"

Wiley smiled. "It means that if there is reincarnation, no one else would want to come back as Robertson except for Robertson."

Valgooney smiled and took another sip of coffee.

"Intimidation," Wiley said as he set his cup down. "That's what Robertson does best, like calling anyone who tries to make a change a 'communist.' Hell, it would be an honor to have him call me something!" He picked his cup back up, poised to take a sip.

"Who is your group, anyway?"

"Anyone who is sympathetic to our situation."

"Just what is your 'situation,' Mr. Wiley?"

He sighed, put his coffee cup down and said, "We represent a large portion of the gay community throughout the eastern seaboard, a little of everyone from minimum-wage workers to doctors and attorneys. We're not the 'Log Cabin Republicans.' And speaking of them, that's an oxymoron. I won't get into it right now, but that's like saying the slaves loved slavery. Okay, so I'm gay. Does that bother you? Maybe I should have said something in the letter or on the phone, but I find it's much easier to discuss these things in person. That way you can see I'm not some phantom faggot, seducing children or cruising rest stops."

"Are your contributors aware of what your group wants to do?"

"Only the nucleus knows. We're at our wit's end. It's why we thought we would try something else."

"Why me?"

"You're like the Godfather, only you're a gorgeous blond woman; people don't die, but you know how to make things happen."

"That's where you have mistaken me. Kidnapping Robertson is cruel, and it's wrong."

"It's just what Robertson is doing to us."

"You do something to Robertson, and if anyone ever makes the connection back to your group, imagine how devastating that information would be to your cause. Don't do it." She pushed her coffee cup away from her, reached into her blue jeans pocket and pulled out five one-dollar bills, folded. She unfolded the dollars and stuck them under the side of the saucer. "That should cover my coffee and a tip." She pushed her chair back and stood up.

"I'm sorry." Wiley started to rise.

Valgooney leaned over the small table, close to his face, her peace-pendant swinging from her neck and close to the last remains of his coffee. "I understand your frustration, but you have to believe in poetic justice; sometimes it's the only thing to believe in." She left Wiley sitting at the table as she left Fullwood's Diner.

"So," Valgooney said to Lola and Earl, "I think that I persuaded that guy not to go after Robertson."

Lola stopped rocking. "The best cause you ever done was puttin' that postmaster in his place." She started rocking. "You just like your momma and daddy, God res' they souls.

Your daddy made trailers; you make causes. I ain't saying you always right, but you sure ain't wrong. 'Different' your middle name." She stopped rocking. "Your daddy and them *damn double-long* trailers."

Yes, those "damn double-long"—not double-wide—silver trailers. The trailers. The building fiasco that her father and Earl had designed and built. People weren't used to it. Most people said it looked like a silver train, not a home. They wanted double-wides. "Double-wides," they said, "look like homes." Sales were slow. The contract her father had brokered with the Myrtle Beach Air Force base to build six hundred trailers was rescinded after the unveiling.

"Looks like a submarine," one of the captains had told him. "We're the Air Force, not the goddamn Navy."

She was still living in the original one—hoisted several years ago onto a fourteen-foot-high foundation. The contractor thought she was crazy.

"You sure you want to go to all this trouble just for a trailer?" he asked as he took off his black baseball cap and scratched his balding head. "You got such a nice piece of land here, why, we could build you a masterpiece."

"I already have a masterpiece."

"It's your dollar, lady," he said, and he scratched his head before he put his cap back on.

Lola had said, "Now it look like it a train on an overpass. Why you go and do that?"

Earl told Lola, "It look fine the way it is."

Lola acted like she was going to work herself into another mad. Valgooney wondered why Earl didn't agree more with Lola when they were all together because she had the feeling that he probably agreed to everything when they were alone. Maybe that's why Earl would make comments to Valgooney when they were all together, just to test the control waters. Sometimes she wondered if Lola treated Earl like that because they weren't able to have children. They had thought about adopting, but before they could go for their first scheduled interview in Charleston, they found out that Valgooney's parents were missing and presumed dead.

The Coast Guard found their boat overturned with a couple of life jackets floating nearby but nothing else.

The captain of the Coast Guard squad stood in the hull of his vessel, looking at the Gores' overturned boat. He shook his head, removed the toothpick that hung over his bottom lip, secured between the slight space on his two front bottom teeth, and said, "This here looks like a case of just plain negligence. I don't know how many times people got to be warned before they wear those damn life jackets. That's why we call them 'life jackets.' My guess is that these here people didn't have any on." Then he stuck the toothpick back between the gap of his teeth.

Her parents were cavalier like that—not wearing life jackets and speeding through the channels, causing wide wakes and laughing the entire way. The only time they were careful was during the busy season. Her father would say, "Too many novices out there; too many unnecessary accidents."

Sometimes it wasn't just the novices. The seasonal summer "hotshots" were the worst. She had seen one of the hotshots, just last season, with two other young men, as they sped through the channel on their Jet Skis. As they zoomed by, the waves, quickly formed by their speeding, slapped onto the shore, causing everyone who was fishing to have to reel their lines back in and recast.

When the guys zoomed by a fifth time, one of the fishermen, who had a pole—the kind used for deep-sea fishing—cast his line just as the lead hotshot barreled through the channel again. The fisherman hooked the young man in the shoulder of his wet suit. As the Jet Ski went flying off without him, the young man landed on his back in the water.

At least fifty people standing along the channel applauded. Their applause infuriated the young man. He swam to a shallow portion of the channel, and when he could, he stood up and shook his fist at the fisherman whose hook was still in his suit. He fumbled with the zipper in the front and was able to pull it down far enough so he could turn the suit around and take the hook out.

"I'M CALLING THE POLICE, ASSHOLE!" His voice echoed across the channel and into the crowd and condos.

One of the young man's friends dragged the defunct Jet Ski through the water for his friend.

"I'M GOING TO BEAT THE HELL OUT OF YOU!" And he zipped his suit up and tried to start his Jet Ski.

The fisherman calmly began reeling in his line.

"DID YOU HEAR ME, ASSHOLE? I'M GOING TO BEAT THE HELL OUT OF YOU! I'VE GOT LOTS OF WITNESSES THAT SAW HOW YOU TRIED TO KILL ME! SOMEBODY CALL THE POLICE!"

He tried to start his engine again, but it was flooded.

As if someone had suddenly warned them to evacuate, everyone who was fishing or lying in the sun began packing their belongings and left.

By the time the hotshot got the Jet Ski started again, the last car was driving away from the public parking space.

Valgooney marveled at how quickly the crowd dispersed, especially the summer crowd. They were infamous for staying on the beaches and on the channel from six o'clock one morning to three o'clock the next. She often wondered what the lure was—at least the kind of lure that most of the people at the beach seemed attracted to: drinking themselves into an all-day stupor, reading trash novels as they blared their music. Almost as bad as their noise and garbage was the parade of bodies: people oblivious to how far their bellies hung down over in their swimsuits, and mounds and mounds of fat on their arms and legs. Valgooney thought their fat looked like heated brie.

Julie E. Townsend

Sometimes she liked to study them, thinking that the vacationers came not for something, but to be on vacation from something. Maybe that's why they didn't care about flaunting loud music and loud fat. Mostly, though, she counted the days until after Labor Day, waiting for them all to go home, because their visits meant noise and trash.

Her parents didn't care much for the crowds, either. But when they were alive, the crowds weren't as thick or as bold. Her parents were the bold ones.

Three days after finding their overturned flat-bottom boat, the Coast Guard called off the search. Earl didn't, though, not even after the Coast Guard found some shredded strips of clothing with a shark's tooth stuck in a buttonhole.

She could see it in Earl's eyes—eyes like dirty pond water—when he finally gave up hoping. He docked the boat on one of the four docks they shared.

Valgooney, who was six then, leaned against a post that was swaying and creaking with the current. Earl tied the boat to another post and cut off the engine; his usually light chocolate eyes looked liked dark caves. They reminded Valgooney of the time her parents had taken her to Linville Falls in North Carolina. Some of the caves and caverns were beautiful when the guide's light shone on them, but one cave, "Death's Darkness," was so deep, she remembered feeling swallowed by something she couldn't touch.

After the will was read and probated, Social Services tried to contest it. Wayne Simmons, director of Social Services, told Earl, "There ain't a court in all of Carolina that's gonna let a colored couple get custody of a Caucasian."

"I understand you and your wife are hoping to adopt. The agency you've been dealing with in Charleston doesn't take too kindly to having mixed families."

Simmons did his best, she supposed, at what he thought was his "duty." He leaked the custody story to the press. One of the people interviewed claimed, "Cole Gore was an odd bird—just look at what he designed to live in." Another person, who refused to be identified, commented, "We ceased doing any future business with him when he refused to alter the design of the trailers. He may have been a good builder, but he's kooky."

It was just the kind of information Social Services needed to show that the Gores were not in their right minds when they appointed Earl and Lola guardians. Simmons thought his trump card—the incident that showed the Gores had to be crazy, and the thing he hoped would ignite the right kind of fire—was when Simmons was quoted in the paper as saying, "Nobody in their right minds would have left their daughter with a colored couple."

After the hearing, when no one else was within earshot, Simmons asked Earl and Lola, "Why are y'all even bothering?"

Lola smoothed the collar of her dress and clutched her left hand tighter around her purse—all signals that she had left simmer and was on high—and pointed her index finger at Simmons, who became transfixed on her finger like it was a gun shooting out words instead of bullets.

"Mister Social Services, you ain't nothin' but some high-wheelin', trouble-causin', tryin'-to-get-promoted, oversized bigot! Heard of Bill Richardson, New York City?"

Not waiting for his answer, but still keeping her finger fixed on Simmons, she turned to Earl. "Honey, anything you wanna add?"

"Think you 'bout say it."

Lola said "Humph," and held Earl's hand. They walked out side-by-side, foot-to- foot, like they were an army, marching out of the building.

Bill Richardson, who had gone to college with the Gores, flew in from New York. It took only one hour of Richardson's laughing boisterously at everything Social Services attempted to point out for the judge to rule there wasn't a case. But before the judge made his ruling, Richardson, after

Julie E. Townsend

laughing at every point, like a spigot, suddenly turned it off. He stopped laughing.

"If you folks would like to take your mumbo-jumbo case all the way to the Supreme Court, I'll be glad to accommodate you because I'm sure the justices will find it even more ludicrous than I." He stood up and straightened his black tie, although it didn't need to be straightened. "The best part of my business is that you never get tired of the bullshit. It's always the same bullshit but different texture."

He left the room, and Earl followed him out into the lobby.

"Guess they ain't gonna be a problem no more," Earl said.

Richardson smiled. "Unless they're bigger idiots than I think."

The locals, however, made it unbearable in other ways. It didn't help matters when the insurance agent, after delivering the proceeds from the settlement, drove to Dock's, a bar near Cherry Grove, and proceeded to get drunk off of shots of vodka. Several people, dancing to beach music, heard how he had met the Jenkinses and Valgooney at Southern National Bank and gave them a check for slightly over one million dollars.

They heard all of the whispers: "rich, uppity niggers," and "crazy white people."

Every once in a while, when Earl would walk her home after dinner, he would joke about how pleased Simmons would be if he only knew she wasn't "sleepin' over with the black folk."

But she knew that she and the Jenkinses still fed the town gossip. Too many conversations ended too abruptly, too often, their voices suspended in the air like cartoon bubbles. Sometimes she tried to pop the bubble with a look; mostly, she was tired of feeling like giving a damn, especially when she heard whispers of "There's that woman who lives in that trailer."

She had been told not too long ago that pilots often used her trailer, which they dubbed the "Silver Bullet," for a marking point. They said it shimmered in the sun and glowed in the moon.

Tonight, by the time she would leave Earl and Lola's, the moon would rise across the water. Sometimes it looked as if the moon were sitting directly on top of the ocean with its white beam waving across the water. Sitting on top of the dunes was her favorite spot to watch the moon. Unfortunately, she didn't have a view from the Silver Bullet. But as she thought *unfortunately*, she knew it was also fortunate that her place was far enough inland on the island, protected by thick brush and thousands of trees, so even though hurricanes had blown through the area too many times to count, the double-long trailer, hoisted up fourteen feet tall and all, still stood, intact. It had even weathered Hugo, the worst of the hurricanes she could remember. But tonight was clear, and she was thinking about destroying a few cages.

Sometimes she'd chance freeing the crabs during the day, but mostly she'd comb the channels at night when the tourists, burnt from the sun, stomachs swollen with too many beers and trips to the buffet, were all too fried to even turn down the sheets of their made-up beds in overbooked hotels.

After she had destroyed as many cages as possible, she'd maneuver the boat back into the main channel and look for wherever the moon lay on top of the water. She'd cut off the engine and throw out the anchor, letting the boat rock to the water's mood. That's when she'd think about her constant dream: the one she had after her parents' boat was found overturned; the dream she had after their funeral; the low-tide dream with sea oats and marshes, seagulls flying low and swooping like helicopters on a mission. And she, lying on her back, gingerly, on a limb of an ancient oak tree, staring into the sky that reflected everything below her like a mirror; her parents walking hand-in-hand toward their boat. How her father untied the rope from the deck, and how as he cranked the motor, the water became sand. They forged through muck, oysters, and crabs—some even pregnant, with their orange bellies dragging across the sand as they scurried to move out of the way.

Still plowing through the sand, her parents made it all the way up the channel to the mouth of the ocean, but when they reached this precipice, the ocean became rippled sand, like layers in an hourglass, but with fingers inside it, shifting.

She wanted to warn them about the gigantic hand that lived above the ocean, sifting sand through its fingers, but she knew they couldn't hear her.

And when she reached this part of the dream, she'd purposely stop the memory, lean over the side of the boat and reel the anchor back in, crank the engine and glide across the water, trying to stay in line with the moonbeam like she imagined the Navy would—that is, if they could ever find honor in navigating by the stars. But nobody relied on the moon and stars to guide their courses anymore. It was radar this and radar that.

Sometimes she wouldn't think about the dream, or the occasional tourist she liked to seduce because they were the easiest to have and to say "good-bye" to. But she'd think about Joe, the only man she hadn't wanted to seduce as compensation for her usual urge that rocked her like her dock did when the tide came in; or what it felt like walking waist-high in the water, sometimes stopping to plant her toes in the sinking sand, pretending she was stronger than the current or the rip-tide that killed her parents—the same thing she felt when she ran her long-distance, twenty-one-mile run from the end of Cherry Grove to Windy Hill and back again, and look for the nameless "him," lying in the sun, slowly browning like the roasted meat she had quit eating a long time ago.

Sometimes she went to their rooms, but mostly she would take them to "The Heart of Cherry Grove," a cheap hotel that had a huge heart painted on the outside of each door. She always paid with cash, and she insisted that her soon-to-be instant lover meet her at the back door to the room.

When she slept with them, she never pretended that they loved her. She did it because she liked the way they felt. She knew this wasn't love—love was mental to her. She knew that one day she would fall in love with someone's mind, and then the physical would be a different kind of connection than it was for her now.

The closest she had come to the mental was when she had met Joe at Boulineau's Grocery, in the pasta aisle, away from the roasting bodies and cheap hotels.

"The runner?" he had asked as she picked up a bag of spinach noodles.

She nodded.

"Training for a marathon?" He leaned against his shopping cart.

"Only do it for me," she had said.

"Impressive, either way," he said. "I'm Joe. Joe Marcucci," and he stuck out his hand. "Haven't seen running like that since I watched the New York Marathon. That's where I'm from. Teach at NYU. But I'm here working on a grant for a while."

Maybe that was the difference too, she supposed. She never knew anything about the tourists. She didn't want to know. It was better that way.

Nor had she ever wanted to take anyone in her boat.

Joe, though, would sit in the belly of it, his legs stretched out, and he would wave his arms like he was conducting an orchestra.

"Don't blame anyone but myself," he had said on one of their rides through the channels. "Been in some of the sweetest relationships with the sweetest women, only to find myself choking. The creepiest ones, though, always analyze every goddamm thing. They're the ones looking for how to hook into control. Take this professor I dated. Fine at first since it was during a semester break, but when the semester cranked up and there were papers to grade, lectures to prepare, research, and conferences, she tried to analyze me like she was Sigmund-fucking-Freud, and she wasn't even in the psychology department." Then he ran his hand through his thick black hair, quickly.

"Even thought I was lying about going to a conference. Thought I was going out with someone else. So I fly out, promising I'll call. Know what she did?" He popped the top off of a Coors and took a long gulp.

Valgooney slowed down the boat and looked at him.

"Showed up. Halfway across the damn country. Can you believe that?"

Valgooney shook her head.

"At my conference session, and then tried to pass it off that she only wanted to see my presentation."

He shook his head. "Kept that thing up until I realized one day that all the happy had been sucked out of me. Learned something, though. Got to look for the chameleon. If you can live with the colors, go for it." He took another gulp of beer. "What about you, Val? What's your story?"

She turned off the engine. "I think people spend too much time trying to find a love, be in love, and then not stay in love."

"Yep," Joe said as he tilted the can in her direction as a toast before he took another gulp.

She didn't tell him about the tourists. Maybe she would if he ever came back for another visit. She thought he'd understand—maybe he'd say it was the chameleon in her. She'd try to explain that the tourists came to the Grand Strand for something—and she was only throwing that something back into their faces: an urge without a heart. Maybe he would know about that, especially living in New York City, where tourists invaded the city every day, all year long. In Myrtle Beach, however, it was more seasonal. Only those rare people who didn't like crowds, who loved Nor'easters, who thrived on the cold sea, would come during the winter months. Some of the seasonal vacationers, whom Valgooney had met and seen, came like clockwork every summer season. In some ways, she resented them as much as she did the weekly renters. The seasonal vacationers only came for the crème de la crème of the season. They didn't get a taste of the beautiful cold, windy, isolated days of winter. They came only for what they considered the quality months or weeks.

Joe, however, was different, because he made her feel lonely, and it reminded her of an uninvited, swollen river, poised to drown everything in sight without permission. If it wanted, it could leave the riverbanks, swallow the grass, cross the road without looking both ways, and climb up trees who would swear, if they could, that they never said they were that thirsty.

That's why she knew she was better alone: time to think about her "sins." Not the ones Christians constantly reminded people of, like they were the local police of everyone's souls, via television, radio, book series... *Left Behind*. Not the kind of sins she heard about from a former president who claimed to answer to "a father of a higher authority," or from the Christians who marketed Jesus like a commodity on the New York Stock Exchange and elected themselves to the Board of Directors—Jesus, the silent partner they sent away for an indefinite vacation. She thought more about the sins of seeing things she thought were unjust but did nothing about.

So if that meant broken crab cages, then so be it; a few horses that might not end up as Jell-O or glue; a few maids who finally had the pay and insurance they deserved — then it was worth a night or two in jail. If it meant picking up the cadavers that the Christians tossed aside on their road to "Calvary"—the ones who didn't quite fit their take on what/how/when a "believer" could/would/should act, for a minute or twenty-four hours a day, then she was going to do something about it too.

That's why she had started a support group last spring for those who had been abused in the name of Jesus. She just didn't know that it would cause such an outrage and get on *Oprah*.

God had to look like a Monet: watery, foggy, and smoky. So how could someone claim it was all crystal clear?

By the time she had left Earl and Lola's, she lay on top of a sand dune, with her fingers laced underneath her head, watching a row of cotton-ball clouds rolling across the horizon. She wondered who needed movies or TV, or anything else, to absorb their gnat-sized attention, when all they had to do was watch this: Nature evoked forgotten memories and things they hadn't yet experienced.

Two weeks ago, Valgooney found a partially decomposed bottle-nosed dolphin. When she saw two bullet holes near its beak, she wondered who could have been so cruel. She thought about Don Quixote's saying, "Murder will out," and how the ocean was like that. Eventually, the ocean divulged everything: people's meanness included. She dragged its five-foot body close to one of the dunes and buried it.

The ocean threw things onto the shore, things that people thought had been lost and forgotten, treasured belongings of those who butted against its power: old bracelets washed from bones; tennis shoes from airplane crashes; needles, bottles and sea carcasses. Doing "it" had never felt lonely, though, until she wanted friends and not just someone to seduce. She would tell herself that friendships were organic. But too many times, as she ran along the beach, she wanted to get beyond those gaping glances, to see a different reflection of herself; maybe have a female friend or two, instead of feeling their stares bore into her. It wasn't her fault that their boyfriends' eyes wandered.

She hadn't done it for a while. Not since Joe left to go back to New York. She wouldn't tell him how his friendship made her want more, not more of him, but more; more than the quiet satisfaction she felt when she joined a cause; more than the men she had seduced; more, even, than smelling the ocean and tracing moonbeams with her fingers as she lay on top of a dune. More of something she couldn't describe. This "more" eluded her like she had eluded the Coast Guard. They didn't know what they were really after, and right now, neither did she.

Julie E. Townsend

WALKING ON WATER

L eslie opened the door to room number 312 at the
Hartford Motor Inn—the place that wasn't as redneck
as the hotel two blocks away, with the hearts painted
on the outside of each door, as if that alone could give the
place some ambiance. It was the kind of place, she thought,
where people would probably go to have a quick "at-it,"
or maybe the kind of room some people would think was
luxurious; that is, if they lived in a mobile home.

At least the place was clean, quiet and reasonably priced,
and it was beginning to feel comforting after six weeks: a
place where she could hide after working all day on the
deal. *The deal.* The deal that would make her the number-one
salesperson, male or female, on the entire eastern seaboard
for at least that year, despite the plunge in the market since
2008. The deal she knew she couldn't do tonight, not after the
aborted dinner at Morton's, and not after the conversation
with Squirrel at the gay bar added to her anger.

Yes, the deal she pieced together, birthed on a fully-
functioning-brain-cell whim, when she was supposed to be
on vacation, crabbing with her mother. She had stood in the
gunk that day….

It wasn't sand; it wasn't dirt: just this soil that looked liked something at the bottom of an abandoned water well, or maybe hell, for that matter. Whenever she took a step, she had to squeeze her toes together tightly so she wouldn't slide out of the blue flip-flops her mother loaned her and land in the gunk. Everywhere she looked, light gunk or deep gunk, small sand crabs darted in and out of holes with openings the size of the head of Q-tips. She didn't want to go crabbing, but to appease her mother, she decided she could stand a few hours of it; anything to ward off their little wars. Besides, she thought, it's not as if they did that much together anymore. Mostly, her mother played golf and lunched at the Rosemont Country Club with a few of her friends who had also retired near Myrtle Beach.

"Mother, I think we've caught enough, don't you?"

"Let's try to catch a few more," her mother said. She was also standing in the gunk, but it didn't seem to faze her. She was holding a thin, partially muddy string that was halfway in the water, halfway in the gunk, with the excess string wrapped around the palm of her right hand. Occasionally, as she moved her hand, her thick gold diamond ring would catch the sunlight.

From where she was standing, Leslie could see the chicken neck secured to the string by a piece of metal. It looked like a gigantic paper clip, but instead of holding together some executive's corporate treatise, this thing was hooked into one of the necks Earl Jenkins had given her that morning.

Earl owned Earl's Fish Bait and Tackle Shop on Main Street in Cherry Grove, right before the street veered off onto Highway 17. Since Boulineau's Grocery was out of chicken necks—the bait her mother insisted on for crabbing—Leslie drove until she saw Earl's sign. Its white-and-blue wooden façade, with a huge red crab painted near the front door, fit in with the motif of a beach town.

She could smell dead fish even before she opened the door to his shop, and when she did, it took her a moment to adjust from leaving the hot, bright morning summer sun to entering the dark, dank cool of his store.

A tall, slim black man with short gray hair greeted her as soon as she opened the screen door. She wasn't sure if he was Earl, but when her eyes adjusted to the dark, she saw a glassed picture frame of a newspaper clipping with his picture, hanging on the wall directly behind him. The headline read: "EARL OPENS FISH MARKET." She noticed that he had on the same shirt he was wearing in the picture. At least it looked like the same shirt: a short-sleeved black button-down. His skin was almost as dark as his shirt. Next to that picture, she saw a yellowed newspaper clipping: "COLORED COUPLE GETS CUSTODY OF CAUCASIAN." It was a picture of Earl with a squat black woman standing next to a willow-thin blond girl.

"How you today?" Earl asked. He was standing behind a waist-level, glassed-in refrigerator, reading a newspaper. He folded the paper over.

"Fine, thank you. Do you have any chicken necks?" Leslie walked closer to the counter.

"Must be goin' crabbin'." He laid the newspaper on top of the cooler.

"Yes sir."

"Lately, 'cause of somebody destroying the cages, we've had a run on necks. But you in luck today. Got plenty of neck. How many you goin' need?"

"I don't know."

"How many goin' crabbin'?"

"Just my mother and I."

"Only goin' need four neck." He reached behind the counter and pulled out two medium-sized plastic bags. He slid his right hand into one of the bags and used his left hand to put the necks in the other bag.

"When it get soggy and the skin start flappin' everywhere, use a fresh one."

"Okay. How much will that be?" Leslie unzipped the top of her dark blue purse and reached inside it for her wallet.

"You on vacation?" He took his hand out of the bag and sealed the one with the necks by pressing together the blue and yellow strip that ran the length of the bag.

"Sort of." But she didn't tell him that two days ago, a deal she had worked on for a year fell apart two hours before the closing. The sellers forgot to divulge that they knew they had asbestos ceiling tiles in every one of the fifty-five apartment units, and they weren't going to have it removed or encased. So Leslie and the buyer walked away from the closing table—and Leslie away from a seventy-five-thousand-dollar commission: her only income for the year, thus far, and more months of eating away at her home equity line and jacking her credit cards up to Jesus. Why she bought that BMW was a question she asked herself every day. She knew better than to count on a commission until the deed was recorded.

That's when Leslie decided a short vacation at the beach with her mother might soothe her, even if she had kept her visits with her at a minimum for too many years to remember. Sure, there was Christmas and the birthdays, and Mother's Day: a token, a tour of duty served by her mother's only daughter and only child.

Her mother, as if in an attempt to make up for all of her workaholic years, invited her to stay. She had even cooked dinner last night, something she hadn't done in years.

Earl said, "Tell you what, go on and catch some crabs on me." He laid the bag on top of the cooler.

The pinkish-white necks reminded her of some of the people lying out on the beach in the morning. By the end of the day, they looked like Earl's painted red crab sign.

"Are you sure? It's not my first visit to Cherry Grove. My mother lives here." Leslie was still holding her wallet.

"Where she stay?"

"Three houses from where the mouth of the channel merges with the ocean, across from that private island."

"Know that spot. Mouth of the channel be the best place for crabbin'."

"That's what she said too."

"Oughta be able to catch a mess of crabs there, but don't forget, if the crab less than five inches across the claw span, throw it back, 'cause it agin' the law." Earl stood straight up when he said this, his eyebrows slightly raised.

Leslie nodded and reached for the bag. "Excuse me?" she said.

Earl hadn't moved at all except that his eyebrows weren't raised anymore.

"Do you know who owns that land across the channel? It makes the rest of Cherry Grove look like one big hotel."

"That the truth. A friend of mine own it."

"Think that he would ever sell it?"

"'He' a she, and no, I don't. She wait until it sunk into the ocean 'fore she go and do that."

"I can see it from my mother's deck. Is it as pretty as it looks?"

"Prettier. Some of the finest land around. Look good 'cause she don't be messin' with it."

"What's her name?"

"Valgooney Gore."

"Valgooney Gore? What an unusual name."

"Name fit."

"What do you mean?"

"Some people meant to walk on water. She one of them." Earl smiled.

"Does she ever let anyone on the island?"

"Nope. Don't even think about it. She have you arrested 'fore you can say your first name. Seen the signs, ain't you?"

Before Leslie could answer, Earl continued.

"It say: '$500 fine for trespassin'.' That a hefty fine to pay for a little explorin'."

"She sounds like she loves her privacy."

"She do."

"Sounds like heaven to me." Leslie started to turn around.

"Even paradise come with a price."

Leslie pivoted back toward him and could have sworn his eyes were watery. "Doesn't everything?" she said.

Earl nodded.

Leslie held up the bag of necks. "Thanks again."

"Come back anytime." Earl reached for the newspaper and unfolded it as Leslie walked out the door.

So as she stood in the gunk facing Valgooney's island, using Earl's necks, she could see her mother's three-story house. She had retired in some style, even if it was only Cherry Grove. Real style would have been Charleston or Kiawah, but Cherry Grove was nice enough. To the right of her, though she couldn't see too far down what people called "The Strand," there were countless beach homes, high-rise condos, old motels, and the Cherry Grove Pier. After Hurricane Hugo demolished it, Mrs. Prince, the owner, rebuilt it.

"I think I have another prospect," her mother said, as if the crab were going to buy a house. Maybe that's why her mother was so successful: Everyone, everything, was a potential transaction.

"See him sneaking up on the right?"

"All I can see is the chicken."

"He's going to make an offer." She slowly began pulling in the line, wrapping the string around her palm. Without moving the rest of her body, not even her head, and barely her mouth, her mother whispered, "Leslie, grab the net."

"You know I'm not any good at scooping them up in the net. You do it. Let me reel him in."

"Okay, but hurry. I'm getting close to closing the deal," she said in a half-whisper, her words seeping from her mouth like air out of an air hose. She slowly wrapped the string around her palm, her eyes transfixed on the water, as if by looking she could control the crab's destiny.

"Mother, he's not a client." Sometimes Leslie wondered why her mother had sold the company when she did, especially since she still referred to everything in real estate terms. But Leslie knew it was a good deal, even though her mother had promised her several times that one day the company would be hers—that if she would go to college and get a business degree and a real estate license, it could all be hers.

When her mother used to talk about the future of the company, Leslie would imagine the day it would be hers and how the newspaper would feature a story about them on the front of the business section with headlines reading, "Mother Bequeaths Top Company to Daughter."

But that didn't happen.

"Everybody, I have something to say," her mother had said that night, on the deck overlooking the backyard of the perfectly manicured two-acre estate in Eastover, one of the most exclusive neighborhoods in Charlotte. All of the cousins, aunts, uncles and even the babies instantly quieted. Her mother had that kind of presence; she always had, even though she was a petite woman. Leslie used to say to those who marveled at how petite she was, "But she has a tall personality."

"As you know," her mother began, "I've always detested being a part of any of the franchises, with their matching colored jackets and badges like they are serving fast-food real estate." She paused for a moment as everyone laughed. "But just last week, Real World Realty made me an offer I can't refuse. In two weeks, the final documents will be drawn, and Ryan Real Estate will officially become 'Real World Realty.'"

Leslie leaned against the deck because suddenly she thought she might throw up.

But that was six years ago.

Leslie laid her string down in the gunk, and as she did, several sand crabs jumped over the string as if they were playing jump-rope at school. Leslie walked over to where the sand ended and the gunk began. She leaned down and picked up a net with a two-foot metal handle and walked back to where her mother was standing. "Here," she said as she held out the metal portion of the net. "Give me the line."

Her mother slid the wad of string off of her palm. Leslie didn't bother to unravel it but instead put the entire wad of string in her hand.

"You're going to mess up the line."

"No, I'm not." Leslie began pulling in the line.

"Don't pull it so fast."

"I'm barely moving, mother."

"Shhhh." Her mother walked slowly into the water and gunk. "I see him. Bring him in just a little closer. Let's get him under contract."

Leslie rolled her eyes as she pulled the string in a few more inches.

Her mother plunged the net into the water and jerked it from the water and up into the air. "Got him!"

As the crab clung to the net, her mother smiled at Leslie, walked over to the yellow bucket where they had put the other crabs and turned the net upside-down into the bucket. "Come on. Let go. You've already committed to the deal." She shook the net hard, and Leslie turned to watch just as she heard the crab crash into the bucket.

Leaning over the bucket, her mother said, "That's the biggest deal today."

"How many more do you want to catch?" Leslie asked as she tried to unravel her string.

"Two more. Then we'll have plenty for my Crab and Artichoke Dip, and then some. You've had that, haven't you?"

"Not homemade."

"Or home caught," her mother added as she smiled and looked down into the bucket again.

"Wouldn't it be easier if you used an underwater crab cage?"

"I had one. But somebody has been destroying the crab cages. Besides, it's more fun catching them this way, don't you think?"

"It's all right except for the heat and the gunk." Leslie wished she had worn lighter clothes. Maybe a white T-shirt and shorts would have felt cooler than the dark blue top and shorts she had on. She could feel sweat rolling between her breasts, down her stomach and into her bellybutton like a newly formed puddle after a torrential rain.

Leslie made sure the chicken neck was secure on the hook and tossed it back into the water. She heard it plop as it landed. "I guess that neck is good for another crab or two. The owner of Earl's told me to change it after a while."

"You didn't go to Boulineau's?"

"They were out, so I drove down Main until I saw Earl's sign. Nice man. He told me a little about the island and its owner." Leslie nodded toward the island.

"She's a strange bird." Her mother shook her head.

"In what way?" Leslie had always despised the way her mother assessed people so quickly. Maybe it worked in sales, she thought, but not when it came to soul.

"She just is." Her mother unhooked the neck from her line and tossed it as far as she could into the channel. Then she bent over and let the water lap her hand. She wiped it on the side of her pants and turned to look at Leslie.

"How?" Leslie asked.

"Sometimes I see her in the distance when she crosses the channel at low tide. Haven't seen her for a while, though.

Not since spring." Her mother walked over to the cooler and pulled out another neck.

"That makes her strange?"

"I can't explain it. She's just so...antisocial."

"Sounds like a plus to me."

"It's not if you want to make it in this world."

"Doesn't look like she's hurting without the world." Leslie pulled the string in a few inches and wrapped the excess around her palm.

"Think what you want, but we all need people. People are important. Remember Barbra Streisand's song? You do know which song I'm referring to, don't you?" Her mother walked back to where Leslie was standing.

Leslie nodded.

Sometimes her mother liked to accentuate the answer to a question by singing lyrics instead of just answering the question. Why and when her mother had started that quirky habit wasn't known, nor had she really paid much attention to it until Andrea made fun of it. "What does your mother sing when she leaves the closing table? 'Money, Money, Money'? And does she ever rap it?"

Her mother repeated the question: "Don't you know the song?"

"People Who Need People," Leslie said, "But I'm not going to sing it."

Her mother began singing the second line in a soft soprano: "*Are the luckiest people in the world...*"

"I say they're codependent." Leslie shifted her flip-flops in the gunk.

Her mother abruptly stopped singing, giving her a look like she used to when she was thinking about punishing her. But Leslie rarely got in trouble. When she was only ten, while most of her peers were busy playing house, she was already keeping house. This responsibility was thrust on her after her mother divorced her father and decided to sell real estate. Because her mother had excused her father from paying alimony or contributing to Leslie's upkeep in any shape or form—not that he was incapable; it was just a cleaner break this way—Leslie became the "housechild" instead of "housewife."

Leslie also learned words from her mother that other kids never heard: words and phrases like "fiduciary," "liens," "equity," "time is of the essence," and her favorite, "amortization."

Sometimes, for fun, she would call some kid a real-estate word. She especially liked the time she told a boy down the street that he ought to quit "commingling," and that "time is of the essence." He swore for the next two weeks that he never played with himself, let alone quickly.

Leslie loosened the string around her palm and turned toward her mother. "I still want to know why you think she's odd. Have you ever talked to her?"

"No, but I've heard things.... She lives in a trailer when she could afford a house."

"Sounds thrifty."

"And she got some boy in trouble this spring."

"What did she do? Get him pregnant?"

Her mother glared at her. "She practically made him homeless."

"How did she do that?"

"It was in all of the papers. She started some group...."

"I thought you said she was antisocial."

"She is, but for some reason, she started this group, and it caused a huge fight between this boy and his father."

"What kind of group?"

Her mother lowered her voice even though there wasn't another person in sight. "Some anti-Christian group."

"What did they do? Put X's on everything? Cancel Easter?" Leslie laughed.

"It really isn't funny. This boy's father is a famous preacher around here, has his own show and everything."

"How old is this 'boy'?"

"Twenty-two or twenty-three, from what I remember reading."

"Then he's no 'boy.' He's capable of making his own decisions. I think she sounds fascinating." Leslie pulled her line in some more.

"You never could read people too well, could you?" As her mother said this, she stared straight ahead into the water.

Leslie looked at her mother's profile. She could feel her face getting hot, but it wasn't from the sun. She felt like saying, "The only person I've never been able to read is you," but she didn't.

Leslie began pulling in her line.

"Is another one biting?" Her mother sounded excited again, like she did with every deal, every possible way to earn a commission, crabs included.

"No. I just don't want to do this anymore." Leslie kept wrapping the string around her palm until the chicken neck came to the surface and then landed on top of the gunk. After she had taken it off of the metal hook, she tossed the neck back into the water and put the string in a wadded pile on top of the cooler.

As she walked back to her mother's house, she decided she would leave the next morning. Ever since her mother had sold the company, all of their conversations and visits ended at the same point: like a cliff they dared not jump off of. Or maybe they were waiting to see who would willingly fall first.

While her mother still stood in the channel crabbing, Leslie picked up the unread *Wall Street Journal* from the kitchen counter, opened the French doors to one of the decks off the back of the house and began reading. An article about Myrtle Beach caught her attention; it described the difficulties the beach had experienced after its Air Force base had shut down.

Julie E. Townsend

According to the article, the base was huge: 3,000 acres, some oceanfront footage, 1,000 apartment units, an airstrip landing, a grocery store, and hangars and offices. Her first thought, as she read, was that it might make a good theme park, timeshare, or interval commercial ownership, but she knew the market was already overbuilt, especially in this huge economic downturn. That was the conclusion of a developer in the article as well, because too many builders had already invaded that beach market years ago, and those who invested couldn't even give their timeshare units away. The theme park wouldn't work, either; but what would work, she thought, would be an industry that needed a place that functioned like a city within a city. She could promote it as adding to the local economy and maybe even broker some tax credits for the buyer.

Did the government have its own real estate company, she wondered, or was it too busy taxing and defending to worry about brokering deals? She laid the paper on the lawn chair next to where she was sitting.

Maybe she would stay another day or two after all. Tomorrow she could go to the county courthouse and find out the property specs on the base, and then figure out whom to contact in Washington. Forget the Internet; hard-core data required some old-fashioned research. She would visit the public library and look up companies that housed their employees for various periods of time—those companies that had vast holdings in real estate, capital, stock, and/or pensions. She glanced back at the newspaper. Sometimes she got her ideas this way; sometimes they panned out, most often they didn't. But if she didn't follow it through, she would be mad at herself. Besides, she still was a deal in the hole. What was one more?

She walked back into the house and called her office in Charlotte.

"Havelock Properties."

"Susan, this is Leslie."

"Hey. How's it going? Can you hold a second?"

Susan put her on hold.

"Thanks," Susan said as she came back on the line.

"No problem. Is Blake in?" He was her sales manager. Sometimes she thought he looked like Tommy Lee Jones when he smiled, but his smiles weren't friendly like the actor's. When Blake smiled, she envisioned an ice wall that she had given up trying to melt or chip away at several years ago. Sometimes people were worth it—the extra effort of being friendly and, if necessary, kissing their ass with a little fake-icing comment. But not Blake. He wasn't even worth bullshit, necessary or unnecessary, Leslie thought. And because he wasn't, and because they both knew this, the tension sat there, like a blocked highway, traffic mounting on both sides, and road-range drivers gearing up for the first fingered bird.

"He's on another line. Can you hold a moment?"

"Yes."

When her deal fell apart two days ago, he made her feel worse than she already did. "Why didn't you check out the asbestos before?" he had asked, wearing his Tommy Lee Jones face.

"Because they told me it wasn't asbestos, that's why."

"And you believed them?"

Why was he pissed? She was the one who wouldn't make any money.

"They built the goddamn thing. They should know," she had said.

That wasn't good enough for him.

"Leslie, he's off now. I'll put you through."

"Thanks."

"Blake Brown." His voice always sounded like he had a bite of steak in it, like he was sucking its juices as he chewed it, draining it dry before he swallowed.

"Blake, it's Leslie."

"Ready to get back to work?"

"That's why I'm calling. I'm going to work on something down here, so I won't be back for a week. Just wanted to check in. I'll tell you more later. Gotta go." Before he could say anything, she hung up. She was sure her quick check-in irritated him, but that was the most she could do to him at the moment. Besides, no one else in the office talked about their deals. It was the first thing she realized was different from selling residential property. In house sales, everyone constantly talked about their listings. They wanted people to know. But in commercial real estate, the only open thing about the business and the office was the floor plan where she had a small desk in her small cubicle.

She walked over to the huge picture window in her mother's living room. Leslie could see her mother still standing in the gunk. Even though it would be cheaper to stay with her for rest of the week, Leslie decided to call the Hartford Motor Inn, which she could see in the distance. If she could have a few days to see whether her idea panned out, without her mother's intrusion or the risk of getting into an argument about their vast differences, then that was worth the expense. She would explain to her mother that Havelock would reimburse her, so why not have her own space? But that was a lie. How could she tell her own mother that it was exhausting not to be herself when they saw each other? Her mother made it clear how she felt about everything from politics to religion, but whenever Leslie attempted to give her opinion, she was silenced with a glare or an "I hope you know how ridiculous you sound." Sometimes she felt the same way at work, and the only time she could revel in life was in solitude. Did this retreat make her weak? Why didn't she impose her opinions on her mother or the brokers at work, just as they did with her? Leslie shook her head as she thought about this. She walked over to the phone book that was lying on the kitchen counter.

She didn't like to lie, large or small, but sometimes people forced you into it, and you learned to take that lie where it suited you, because maybe that's all you could take at the moment.

"OF THE DEVIL..."

L eslie was surprised that the military base had opened in 1941. And why Myrtle Beach, of all places? Maybe some general thought that as long as he was going to be stationed somewhere, it ought to be pretty. But then again, if she remembered her history correctly, in 1941, everyone in America was paranoid that Hitler might sneak across the Atlantic. That level of paranoia hadn't been felt again until Bush and his post-9/11 WMD claims.

Her first stop was the county courthouse. When she had finished copying all of the tax records, GIS maps, and square-footage numbers of all the buildings and bunkers, she got directions from a clerk to the main library. She needed to look up any articles that had been written about the base, so at least she would know who had already made a play for the property. Then she would spend some time researching companies. You had to know the product first to make sure that it made a good fit, and then figure out for whom. That was the first rule of commercial real estate.

When she walked into the library, the librarian, an older woman with gray hair draped down to her waist, assisted her not only by giving her the latest stack of newspapers, but by telling her that numerous developers had made proposals for it. "They all thought they had the funding lined up, and then, one by one, the deal would fall apart, especially in this market," she said. "Wish somebody would go ahead and make it happen. But no, they've just gotta keep everybody on edge around here. You know, young lady, not knowing something is as bad as knowing, sometimes." And as the librarian said this, she moved her head up and down as if Leslie were agreeing with her.

Leslie took three rolls of microfilm and a stack of newspapers that had not yet been put onto microfilm over to a machine. She decided to look at the microfilm first. While she was scanning the film, an article caught her attention: "REVEREND FARNSWORTH ARRESTED!" She scrolled the film down a little further:

> *The Reverend John Farnsworth, 58, was charged with assaulting his son, David Farnsworth, 23. The Reverend blamed an unidentified woman for "influencing and corrupting" his son with her "devil group." David called his father's accusations "just more religious tripe." He claims the group was only a "support group for children of fundamentalist parents." The Reverend posted the $5,000 bail, and the court date is set for April 25.*

Leslie laughed aloud and quickly glanced around the library. She and the librarian were the only ones there. "So this is what mother was referring to," she whispered to herself. She pushed the print button and continued to scroll through more film:

FARNSWORTH'S SON GOES ON *OPRAH*
David Farnsworth, 23, son of the Reverend Farnsworth, whose syndicated show, "Jesus 4 U," is seen in 65 cities across the country, will appear on Oprah, *Channel 7, in response to the charges that were brought against his*

Julie E. Townsend

father. David dropped the charges of assault and battery because, he said, "If I learned anything at all after hearing the old man preach for all my life, it's that you've got to forgive people." The assault occurred when the Reverend allegedly beat David because he was attending a support group started by Valgooney Gore, 38, of Cherry Grove. Gore could not be reached for comment, but David said she was making the group national. The Reverend Farnsworth claims the group is "of the devil," but David said the group is needed. "Too many people have abused Christianity for too long. She only wants to put the 'Christian' back into Christianity."

Leslie got up from the screen and walked to where the librarian was reshelving some books. She was squeezing a red-bound book between two others.

"Excuse me. Did you see the *Oprah* show when Farnsworth's son was on it?" The woman laughed. "That was the best news around here for weeks and weeks. You know, not much ever happens around here. Maybe a tourist gets a shark nip, and sometimes the bikers' convention gets wild, but that Farnsworth kid won it all." She stood smiling past Leslie like she was watching it over again in her head. "I recorded it." And when she said this, it sounded as if she had just accepted an award.

"Any chance I could watch it here?"

Ignoring Leslie's question, the librarian turned around and went over to a desk. She sat down.

Leslie didn't know if she should stand there or go back to microfilm.

"Ta da," the librarian said, and she waved a disk. "I'll set you up on a DVD player, and you can watch it here." She shook her head. "Best news around."

"Was Valgooney Gore on the show?"

"You mean the instigator? No. She's a recluse, you know."

"I don't know anything about her except that she owns an island in Cherry Grove."

"It was sad about her folks," the librarian said as she grabbed the handle of the book cart and moved it back and forth an inch, while she held the disk in her other hand. "They moved here from Alabama with a black couple in the early sixties. Some folks in the area didn't like such a chummy black-and-white friendship. After all, it was the sixties."

Leslie thought, *And she thinks that's changed?* No wonder people couldn't get past their prejudices with gays. They were still stuck on skin.

"Her folks went out fishing one day, and a bad storm came up out of nowhere." Leslie noticed how the librarian began rocking the book cart back and forth.

"Coast Guard found their boat overturned, but they never found their bodies." She shook her head. "Folks were smart, though. Had every bell and whistle on two insurance policies. Valgooney became a millionaire when she was just a little thing, but the real kicker was that they had left explicit instructions for their black friends to be her guardians." The librarian laughed. "I remember all of that fuss like it was yesterday.

"It made sense to me, I mean because they were friends and neighbors. Their land is all connected. The only thing that separates them is a three-foot channel." The librarian stopped rocking the book cart.

"No one heard anything about her for quite some time until she started setting up various foundations and organizations. If you want to know anything more, you could try reaching the reporter that worked on the Farnsworth story. You can get his name from the byline."

"I appreciate that," Leslie said.

"Come on back here, and I'll set you up on the machine."

OPRAH

L eslie didn't think David Farnsworth looked like much, just some skinny guy with a goofy grin, a thick southern accent, and a spattering of pimples that Oprah's people must have forgotten to cover up. *Guess they only apply the makeup to the stars,* she thought.

While David spoke, he held onto the hand of a young woman who had waist-length blond hair and who didn't look that much older than he. He made a point of telling Oprah and the audience that they owed their falling in love to someone special down in Cherry Grove, South Carolina. "This here is Lucinda." The audience clapped, and Lucinda waved with her free hand.

"David," Oprah began. "Why don't you tell us about the confrontation with your father?"

David shifted in his chair but still held onto the woman's hand. "It was shortly after I had been going to these here meetings that was supposed to be a place where people like me who have fundamentalist parents could go and, you know, let off a little Jesus steam, if you know what I mean."

The audience laughed. Leslie wondered if they were laughing at his thick accent. The camera flashed over to

Oprah, and she smiled. "What sort of things did you do at the meetings?"

The camera did a close-up on David as he responded. "Well, see, first of all, you wouldn't believe how many of us they is. I'm talking bout near fifty people every time we opened the doors."

"Uh huh," Oprah said.

"People just wanted to talk. Talk about how nothing they did was ever right. And I'm not talking about major sins here; I'm talking about how they got a sermon if they chewed their gum on the wrong side of their mouth."

The audience laughed with Oprah.

"Gum chewing is a sin," Oprah said, and then added, "I'm one heck of a gum-chewing sinner, then."

The audience laughed as the camera flashed to David and Lucinda, who smiled.

"Well, you get the point," David said. "Unless you been in that kind of compressed situation...."

"Do you mean 'oppressed'?" Oprah asked.

"Yeah, that's the word. Anyway, until you've been made to feel like you're on a one-way ticket straight to hell unless you believe and do everything they say, then you can't know how the compression, I mean the oppression, eats you alive." David sighed.

"How did you find out about the group?" Oprah asked as the camera stayed on David's face.

"From an ad. It said all interested parties was to write to this P.O. box number, and somebody would call back with the information, but since I was living at home at the time, I wrote and told this whose ever P.O. box thing it was not to call me, but write me back. So the founder did, and I started going to a couple of meetings and all, but when my daddy found out, he was so mad he could've spit me halfway across the United States."

A few people in the audience laughed. Leslie noticed how he was still holding Lucinda's hand as the camera

Julie E. Townsend

scanned the audience and then back to David.

"See, even though I had kept my whereabouts quiet, my daddy is a smart man. Let me rephrase that. He's got friends all over the place. I come home and daddy was sitting around the kitchen table with three of them deacons from the church. I knew then I had entered a snake pit. He says, 'Son, where you been today?' And I say, 'Been walking on the beach." Then he got one of them looks on his face that he gets when he gonna blow some Jesus from his lips, and he says, 'Son, I'll ask you again. Where you been?'

"'Now daddy,' I say. 'Please don't get mad, but I went to check out a group that's kinda like a Bible study without a Bible.'"

The camera panned the audience. No smiles.

Oprah interrupted. "David, we need to break for a commercial. We'll be right back with an interview with David Farnsworth, president of a support group that helps people deal with parents who are fundamentalist Christians."

Leslie fast-forwarded it to where David was talking again and pushed the "Play" button.

"...looked like a big old cloud blew in from the ocean and was looking for some place to land. He says, 'Anything not of the Lord is of the devil.'

"And then he got up from his chair slow-like and nodded to the men still sitting around. 'Only one way to eradicate the harm that has befallen my son. We've got to cast these demons out of him.'

"Oprah, I don't know what came over me, but for once in my life, I stood there tall and all, pointed my finger in his face almost touching his big red nose, and I says, 'Don't you touch me, old man! I'm tired of you and your Jesus!'

"Then he slapped me real hard across my face, and he hit me again and again, until my legs buckled up right under me. So there I was, all sprawled out on the kitchen floor, when all of those deacons started laying their hands on me shouting for the demons to come out. 'FOUL SPIRITS,' they cried, 'COME OUT IN THE NAME OF JESUS!'

"Weren't but one thing to do. Told them the next person who touched me would be reported to the police.

"Daddy turned to one of the deacons who looked like Pat Robertson when he might have seen better days and says, 'Brothers of the Lord, my son is still possessed.'

"The one who looked like old Pat turned to my daddy and says, 'Reverend, he's worse off than we thought.' And he turns toward me, but before he can say anything to me I says, 'Hey you, Deacon Fat BLEEP (David mouthed "fuck"). You really think you're something. Why, you'd probably try to eat Jesus if you could, and I don't mean communion neither!'

"And then they beat the tar out of me. Somehow I got away and I run out of the house like there ain't no tomorrow. Called the police. Whoever answered that phone sure was nice. Asked if I needed an ambulance. I told them 'no' even though my nose was broke and half my ribs."

Leslie pushed the pause button, then fast-forwarded past the commercials and pushed "Play" again.

"So like I was saying, nobody has to put up with abuse from their parents, 'specially if they say they of the Lord and what not. 'Cause I always thought the Lord was about kindness, acceptance and love, but maybe I don't know anything after all."

The audience clapped loudly.

The camera flashed to Oprah again and then to a young, stocky-looking woman in the audience.

"Yeah, how can I join? I'm tired of my mother witnessing to me all of the time. Over and over again. And if I don't go to church, she won't let me eat!"

The camera flashed to Oprah. "Won't let you eat? Maybe I can go on *that* diet." The audience laughed.

The young woman said, "She hasn't starved me yet, but to deny your daughter of meals because you don't want to go to church for the sixth time that week is abuse, if you ask me!"

The audience clapped.

Another young woman in the audience stood up. "I can top her story."

Oprah looked into the camera, "You can?"

"Yes!"

"We have time for one more, don't we?" she asked, again to the camera.

"When I told my parents that I didn't want to go to church anymore—not because I wasn't a Christian, but because I didn't believe that the Bible was God's holy word sent down from almighty heaven—how could it be? It was written by men and tampered with for hundreds of years—they cut me out of the family will!"

Oprah shook her head. "You two women might need to help each other out...no food or future money!"

The audience laughed and clapped at the same time.

Oprah smiled into the camera. "David, any response to this?"

"Well, that's exactly why we gotta help each other. Nobody, and I mean *nobody*, should be punished by their parents like that. Why, I do believe we are in the *U-nited* States of America, and we're supposed to be free, ain't we?"

The audience clapped, loudly, as the camera panned the audience.

"We gonna set up a chapter in every major city across the *U-nited* States. Meanwhile, until it comes to your city, you can use the computer to contact us."

"David," Oprah asked, "is this what you're doing full-time? How do you support yourself?"

David turned and looked at Lucinda and then back at the camera. "We gonna do it like AA does it. Set up chapters and let people fund it themselves. And until all of this gets set up, someone real nice and generous down home is supporting the cause until it's all done. Then who knows? Maybe I'll go back and finish college. Become a preacher."

The audience clapped again.

"Who funds it?" Oprah asked.

David turned to Lucinda again. The camera flashed to their hands. Leslie was amazed at how long they could hold hands.

"I ain't at liberty to say, but she's more generous than any so-called Christian I ever did meet, my daddy included."

"Looks like we need to take another commercial break, and when we return, we'll discuss the problems that are created when public policy interferes with the Bible, or should I say, when the Bible interferes with public policy," Oprah said. The audience clapped.

Leslie stopped the DVD. As she waited for the compartment to open, she thought about Valgooney's idea for the support group. She wondered how much hate mail she had gotten from Christians...the same believers who killed the pro-choicers; the Reverend Phelps from the Westboro Church in Kansas, who had marched during Matthew Sheppard's memorial service holding up signs that read "God hates fags." And how now Phelps had the audacity to show up at the funerals of soldiers returning from Iraq and claim that the reason they were killed was because of America's tolerance toward homosexuals. She shook her head and then looked to see where the librarian was. She knew the librarian would probably want to chat, and just then, Leslie was feeling guilty because she wasn't getting the work done that she had set out to do. Sometimes she got mad at herself when she felt guilt-ridden. But why? She hadn't gone on a real vacation since graduation from college. And that was a long time ago. So as she looked sheepishly around the library again and decided that the librarian must be in the bathroom, she jotted down "Thank you" on a scrap piece of paper and set that on top of the

DVD. She jammed the articles she had copied earlier into her briefcase and left.

With the balcony door open in her hotel room, letting in the muffled murmurs of tourists talking on the ocean front down below, Leslie placed a call to a Major Johnson, the Washington spokesperson for the base whose name she had seen mentioned in one of the articles; but he wasn't in.

"What is this in reference to?" a woman with a squeaky, high-pitched voice asked. Young, Leslie thought. The higher the pitch, the younger they were. Women's voices were like wine: They got deeper and richer with age.

"Tell him Leslie Ryan with Havelock Properties called. He can reach me on my cell at 704-687-2801."

"Will he know what this is in reference to?"

Leslie couldn't stand it when secretaries asked this question. Sometimes she wanted to say, "Only if he's psychic." Where did they come up with their phone responses? The last time a secretary said, "I'm sorry, Mr. so-and-so isn't in," Leslie had said, "You're sorry? I'm the one who wanted to talk to him." At least that secretary had a sense of humor. She doubted high-voice did, so she answered, "The Myrtle Beach base."

"I'll tell him," she said.

"Thank you." Leslie hung up.

THE BOYS

She reached into her briefcase and pulled out the newspaper articles she had copied about the Reverend Farnsworth. Tim Lewis with *The Sun Times* had written the articles. Maybe he would know something about the base, and maybe she could tempt him with a promise to let him be the one to know first if she ended up brokering the deal.

But she was kidding herself. She was intrigued about Valgooney, who sounded like a combination of Mother Teresa and Joan of Arc. And the more intrigued she had felt as she drove back to the Hartford Motor Inn from the library, the more she couldn't swallow hard enough to suppress the lump in her throat...the lump that was always waiting patiently for her when she thought about Andrea. A lifetime wasn't long enough for grief, she thought. She swallowed hard again and decided to divert her own attention.

She looked up the phone number for *The Sun Times* and called.

"*The Sun Times*. How may I direct your call?"

"Tim Lewis, please."

"Hold, please."

A few seconds later, he answered, "Lewis."

"Mr. Lewis? This is Leslie Ryan from Havelock Properties in Charlotte, but I'm in Cherry Grove. Do you have a few minutes?"

"Caught me at a good time. Nobody's being murdered or nothing pillaged, yet."

Leslie laughed. Nice midwestern voice, she thought, but he had a gut—he sounded full when he spoke, like a sack of spuds. "I'm actually calling about two things—one might eventually lead to a story, and the other is to ask you about the Farnsworth story."

She heard his chair squeak.

"I've got an angle on the military base, real-estate-wise."

"Yeah, you and every broker this side of the Mississippi. Disney was here last week."

"I've got a different idea for the deal."

"What?"

But instead of answering him, she asked, "Think Disney will buy it?"

She heard him breathe into the phone. Definitely overweight, she thought.

"We're already theme-parked out. Besides, I think the government is holding out for as much money as possible. You know, they always need more money for their invasions." Then he snorted.

"The other thing I wanted to ask you about is Valgooney Gore." His chair squeaked louder this time.

"What about her?"

"I know she owns 1,000 acres of some of the best land on The Strand."

"If you're looking to approach her about selling, don't bother. In fact, don't bother her at all."

"I was just curious about her, that's all." Leslie felt her face flush quickly, like she had just turned on the shower and it hit her with hot water. She cupped her hand over the receiver because she had to swallow hard.

"You and me both," he said. "I tried to approach her about the Farnsworth story and you know what she said? She said, 'The story is between David and his father, not me.'"

"You've met her, then?"

"Wasn't easy. She about killed me in the process of getting what little information I did."

"Killed you?"

"She's in some kind of shape. Runs I don't know how many miles a day, and if she's not sprinting like some Olympian, she's demonstrating what power-walking really means. Since her number is unlisted, and I knew from the guy who owns Fullwood Diner that she's an early morning exerciser, I waited for her at six o'clock one morning. The tide was real low, so there she was—walking across the channel just like the guy at Fullwood's said she would do. Do you know where I'm talking about?"

"Yes." And Leslie wondered how many times her mother had watched Valgooney cross the channel.

"Then you've probably noticed how the tide can get so low there that you can walk right across from Cherry Grove to her island. That's what tempts people all of the time to trespass on her property, but I already knew that pissed her off, and since I was trying to get a story out of her, I waited. So I watched her walk across the channel. I couldn't decide what was more gorgeous at the moment: the sight of her blond hair blowing back from the ocean breeze and those runner's legs of hers, or how the sun was just beginning to rise over the ocean, making the sand shimmer like diamonds. I called out her name. She nodded and kept walking. I thought I was going to have a heart attack trying to catch up with her. When I somehow managed to catch up with her I said, 'I'm Tim Lewis with *The Sun Times*. How are you?' And she says, 'Mr. Lewis, I'm sure you didn't come all the way out here to ask how I am. And given how hard you're breathing, I doubt you came out here for exercise.'"

Leslie laughed. He had a gut. She knew it. She wiped her forehead. It was moist.

Tim laughed too. "Pegged me all right. Hey, but I respect that. So here I am, huffing and puffing just to keep up with her, and I think I had better get right to the point or else I will pass out. 'Ms. Gore,' I say, 'Are you responsible for starting a support group for children of fundamentalist parents?' She turned and looked at me, one of those once-over looks, and says, 'Mr. Lewis, I know that you were able to get my name from the classified ad billing. And a slight correction, it is a group for anyone who has been traumatized in the name of Jesus, especially by the Evangelicals.'

"So I say, 'Our departments don't merge information.' I wished I hadn't said that because she turned those big blues of hers on me again and says, 'Since when did newspaper companies withhold information from themselves?'

"Of course, I didn't know what to say. So she says, 'Mr. Lewis, what do you see?'

"She's still got the blues on me. I say, 'A beautiful woman who sure can walk fast as hell.'

"She says, 'Since your lungs should be on reserve by now, I'll tell you what you should see, if for some reason the lack of oxygen is thwarting your deductive skills. You should see that if you don't say something worthwhile in about one minute, you will not have any credibility with me.'

"All I can say, she's one tough cookie. You know, I don't know why I'm telling you this story, especially since it makes me look like a wuss. I've wanted to tell someone what it was like to meet her. See, if I told the guys at work, they'd rib me about it for the rest of my days here, but like I said, here I am blabbing it to a complete stranger on the phone. Maybe it's because you're a woman. Does any of this make sense?"

"I think I know what you mean."

"Do you think she hates me?" he asked.

"Why would she hate you?"

"I don't know. Just a feeling. Maybe I'm wrong. After all, it's not like I have to win everybody's heart. I never did get the information I wanted; in fact, she ended up giving me a lecture on the overdevelopment of the Strand and the senseless millions that were being spent to ward off the erosion. She told me if I really wanted to work on a worthwhile story, I should expose the waste spending for the tons of sand for what it was. And then she left me standing in the morning sun as she sprinted off faster than any runner I have ever seen."

"Have you talked to her since?"

"Not since she called me to lambaste me when some reporters from Charlotte interrupted one of their group meetings, after Oprah did a show on it. She thought I had leaked their new meeting place to the press. When she realized she was wrong, she apologized. Now that's classy, because too many people can't seem to utter those simple words of 'I'm sorry.'"

Leslie heard his chair squeak again, almost like he had leaned back in it, exhausted from the story. "Mr. Lewis?"

"Call me Tim."

"Tim, I enjoyed talking with you, but I need to go. I promise to call you if I do anything with the base."

"Fine."

"Good-bye." She heard his chair squeak again, and the phone clicked. She held the phone in her hand for a moment, thinking about her: this woman whom she hadn't met and probably never would. So what if she met some beautiful, eccentric woman? She was probably straight. Just what the hell was she going to say? "Hello, I find you fascinating?" How damn queer, she thought. Maybe that's where the word came from in the first place. She didn't want to look like the fool she was already feeling; like she was back in junior high school. No. You don't do anything with it, she thought. You just keep it inside and deny it, just like you do in the middle of the night when you wake up out of sleep

Julie E. Townsend

and dreams, knowing it's too early to eat, but you're hungry just the same. Hungry for something you haven't had in a long time.

Besides, maybe only Andrea had brought out that hunger.

As she hung up the landline, her cell rang.

"Leslie Ryan," she said in her best business telephone voice. She was often told what a nice voice she had—not heavy with any one particular accent, but slightly southern: the polite, but firm and friendly southern. She learned that from her mother years ago. It always amazed her how her mother could switch into a different voice as soon as she answered the phone. They could have been embroiled in an argument, but as soon as the phone rang, her mother became a different person. Leslie thought it was just a southern thing. An inbred custom. A conditioned fake. She wondered if more southern women faked orgasms than northern women. Maybe southern women just knew how to accentuate it better. God knows they could hold onto words longer, so why not fake orgasms? "Yes!" in a moment of passion would be "Yeeeeeeessssssssss!" to a southerner. Someone should do a study.

"Major Johnson returning your call." His voice sounded young; maybe mid-thirties. There was an edge to it. Young people, especially men, Leslie thought, had to stake out their territory. Older men didn't have to, need to. They had staked for naught before. The major didn't know it yet, she thought.

"Thank you, Major. I'm a broker with Havelock Properties from Charlotte, North Carolina. I understand that you're the contact person for the potential sale of the base in Myrtle Beach. I would like to meet with you at your earliest convenience to discuss how I might facilitate the sale of the property."

"Hold on. Slow down. Who did you say you are with?" She despised it when people asked her this question. They were undermining the credibility that she was trying to establish. She pictured his crew cut bristling like fall wheat blowing in a field.

"Havelock Properties. We deal with investment properties and industrial sites throughout the east. We did that MCO industrial site right outside of D.C. last year. Do you know about that plant?"

"I see." His "I see" stalled on the phone. He was testing her credibility; she could feel it.

That was something she had never dealt with before going into commercial real estate. Before, all she had to say was, "I'm Leslie Ryan with Ryan Real Estate," and people would either respond with "Why, hello,"—the kind of "hello" that had an assumption like built-in appliances and wall-to-wall carpeting—or they would say, "I know your mother. She sold us our first home fifteen years ago." That's what she was used to, not this constant battle of having to prove herself to strangers. Sometimes it seemed more difficult because she was one of the few women in the business. Company-wide, there were only eleven female brokers in fifty states. At Havelock, it was something that scared her at the same time that it inspired her. Sometimes she didn't know what was more pressure-filled: being the only female broker in her office or working for her mother and enduring being dubbed "the boss's kid," with all of its stigmas. It had to be same with preachers and their children, she thought. The expectations were as tall as a skyscraper.

"Major Johnson," she began. "I would like to fly to D.C. and discuss this matter with you and whoever else will be involved. Would either next Tuesday or next Thursday suit you?"

"Tell me what you've got."

"Major Johnson, I never discuss business on the phone, at least not initially."

"I see." His "I see" felt confining, just like her hotel room.

"Major Johnson, our meeting may be premature, but if and when I bring a viable buyer to the table, we'll be that much further along." Leslie felt her heart racing. Sometimes having to make the initial contact still made her nervous, but she had decided a long time ago that she thrived on the rush. It's why she did it. She understood why her mother had always worked so much—she was hooked on the thrill.

"Next week is no good. One o'clock this Thursday. Be here at one."

She thought about saluting and saying, "YES, SIR!" but she didn't. She did, however, stand up straight beside the bed, like she was ready for inspection. "I look forward to discussing this matter with you. Good-bye."

Major Johnson didn't say "good-bye," but she heard the phone click. *You sound like a real sweetheart*, she thought. She set the receiver back on top of the phone and walked over to the table beside the window where she had left her paperwork the day before. She glanced down at the list of potential research companies, but until she had some sort of commission protection, she wouldn't divulge too much.

Getting that first leg of negotiations done was always the topic of conversation in the office: that somebody—whether the buyer or seller or someone with the authority— had to sign a contract guaranteeing that the broker would be paid if the deal closed. And if you didn't get someone to sign on the dotted line, you had just gotten screwed without what the guys in her office called "commission condoms."

She knew that soon she would have to tell Blake what she was doing. She dreaded doing it because she knew he would undermine her somehow, make it his deal, or put some other broker on the deal with her, under the guise that they were there to help her. She knew better. But she didn't know any other way to ward off his power until she was more established.

Five years in the business, and they still seemed opposed to her trying to do some deals on her own. What were they risking? She was the one risking it all to be a success. Would a big deal make them loosen the unspoken hold they kept over her—a hold that choked her out of sleep sometimes on those nights when she obsessed about not feeling accepted? Wasn't her secret about being gay enough punishment?

She felt their distance. Subtle. Subtle as a Dear John letter.

No one had ever invited her to join them for a drink, nor to work out in the gym, like they did with each other every day. Or play golf, go sailing. Nothing. They only seemed capable of having trite conversations with her about how tough the business was or telling her raunchy jokes. It would be nice, she thought, to feel like she could have a friend or two. It wasn't as if she had never had male friends before. Some of her closest friends in college were men. But in college, she was "allowed" to party with the guys, crack the same jokes and cuss like them, if she wanted. But the brokers at Havelock practiced Orwell's "Doublethink."

At first, she tried to break the barriers, like the time the "girls," as the men in the office liked to call the assistants, invited her for a night out: "You know," the office manager had said, "just us girls." So she went out with them, but all they did was complain about having to type up so-and-so's offers or contracts, and discuss who was sleeping with whom.

When she drove home that night, she was pissed. Pissed for how much they bored her. They were like a lot of women she had met: incapable of giving anything beyond surface warmth to other women because, she thought, women used other women to park their loneliness until a man could rescue them. Their loneliness smoldered; its smoke choked her. Not that she would ever tell them, but she knew what it meant to be lonely. She got her B.A. in that when her mother left her alone every weekday afternoon and early evening and most of every weekend as a child. It was good preparation for the loneliness she felt after Andrea's death...

Julie E. Townsend

that's when she appreciated the infinity of the black hole of the universe: an impressive void of nothingness. So the evening with the "girls" at work did triple time: straight-up, shaken, and stirred with anger.

Then she tried the other extreme. She knew the brokers met for a drink every afternoon in a bar on the first floor of the thirty-story building where Havelock was located. Without an invitation, after she had been working there for six months, she stopped by the bar for a drink before going home. There they were, Havelock's finest: Citadel graduates who marched from college to IBM to Havelock, rising in the ranks as self-proclaimed "entrepreneurs." She thought it was odd, or maybe it really wasn't odd, that every broker, with the exception of one guy, had the same background. For a company that claimed it recruited "those with entrepreneurial spirit," they were keen on hiring those they could most easily fit into a mold. She had often heard the expression "cookie-cutter deal" when the brokers were referring to real estate that all looked the same: the strip malls, or the generic Class C office space that was a good deal but lacked any individual distinction. When she would hear them use this expression, she thought they were cookie-cutter brokers: the business equivalents of *The Stepford Wives*.

Sometimes she visualized a pile of white dough rolled out to perfection, their faces on the mold pushed into it and then baked to a crisp, completed with fixed, forced, practiced expressions.

When she entered the bar, a couple of the brokers nodded in her direction, but no one made an effort to join her. She politely moved through the after-work crowd to the bar.

"What can I get for you?" asked the redheaded bartender, who wore tight black jeans and a low-cut blouse. The bartender looked like she had on a Wonder bra, Leslie thought. No one was that taut at her age, with breasts jacked up like a car getting its two front tires changed.

"A Cabernet, please."

"Mondavi all right?" the redhead asked as she poured a draft with one hand and stuffed dollar bills in the cash drawer with the other.

"That's fine. Oh, and can I have a napkin so I can throw my gum away?"

"Eight dollars, honey. Wanna run a tab or pay now?"

"Pay now, and may I have a napkin please?"

The bartender didn't hear her ask about the napkin. She tried to ask her again, but the bartender was too busy trying to take orders, mix drinks, and punch in credit card numbers, so after she had paid for the drink, she moved away from the bar. For a moment, she couldn't decide whether she should walk over to where the brokers were standing or stay where she was—wedged close to the bar between a stool and three other people. As she scanned the bar looking for more elbow room, she saw James, one of the brokers, hunkered in the corner of the bar with Mike and Bob like a football squad. James motioned for her to come over.

"So Les, how goes it? Still like this business better than selling houses?" James asked. He was a Citadel graduate, who always stood like he was at attention, ready to salute. "We were just wondering what you thought about Blake's comment this morning in the meeting." James quickly looked over at the other brokers and then back at Leslie.

"Which comment?"

"The one about having to make sure you always have a commission agreement up front because you don't want to get your tit caught in the ringer." James laughed. So did the other brokers.

Leslie took a sip of wine and almost swallowed the gum she kept meaning to throw away. "I'd rather have a pap smear." She took another sip of wine.

No one laughed and instead they all looked down at their shoes at the same time. Bob was the first to break the silence.

"So, what's your story? Have you been married, divorced, single or what?"

"Single." Leslie took another sip. Why did people always ask this question? Did that really give someone self-worth either way? If it wasn't that question, it was "What church do you go to?" The next time someone asked her that question, she was going to say, "I'm home-churched." Maybe that would shut them up. But her colleague didn't ask the standard southern follow-up question.

"Bet some sellers would love to do a deal with you," Bob said.

Leslie took a sip of her wine before answering, "I hope so, or else I won't be in this business long."

"Say, Les." James took a swig from his Miller beer. "The boys were just talking before you came in about how being a woman really is an advantage in this business. What do you think?"

"If it is, I don't know it yet."

"All you would have to do is flaunt your stuff a little more, and I bet you could get an appointment with anyone in town. Now, Bob here's too damn ugly to get an appointment; his wife won't even do him, but you, hey." Bob gave James a punch on his shoulder.

"What we're trying to say," James smiled and continued, "is a woman should use everything she can to her advantage. A guy can't do that. Well, he could, but then someone would probably think he's a fag or something. So use it. Show it, shake it, whatever." He leaned his head back and laughed. "Damn, sometimes I wish I were a hot-looking woman."

"Why?" Bob asked "So you can screw your way to the top?"

Mike, the other broker who had not said anything up to this point, laughed. "That's what a woman did at IBM. And then when she didn't get the position she wanted, no pun intended, she filed a sexual harassment suit. Women got us coming and going."

Leslie took another sip of wine. She felt flushed but she wasn't sure if it was the wine on an empty stomach or that she was beginning to feel a strong, self-righteous, pissy moment coming on.

"Women are lucky that way, you know." James tilted his beer bottle in a toast of agreement with Mike. "They're the ones who really rule the world."

"Yeah, we're real *lucky*," Leslie said. "We get to put up with sexual comments all day. And if we ward them off, we're called a 'cold bitch,' and if we don't, we're called a 'slut.'"

Bob grabbed her elbow and leaned in close to her. She could smell gin on his breath. It reminded her of prickly pine needles. "What about you Leslie, are you a good broker or a bad broker?"

She stepped back a few inches, but he didn't loosen his grip. "What do you mean?"

He leaned closer than he had before, so close that she could feel his breath on her ear. She watched his martini slosh. "A slut?"

As she looked around their semicircle and saw the other brokers smiling, she gaped and almost dropped her gum.

That's when she decided to do it. She took the gum out of her mouth and dropped it into his glass. It hit the olive and sank to the bottom: the olive bobbing up and down like apples in a water barrel.

Bob clinched his jaw and said, "I can't believe you did that."

Leslie put the wine glass to her mouth and took another sip. She didn't look at them until she moved the glass from her mouth, and then in half toast gesture, she said, "Goodnight."

"Nice talking with you, Les." James said.

"Thanks again," Bob said, and he tilted his drink toward her. "It was just a joke, you know."

Julie E. Townsend

Leslie saw a table by the door. "So was that," she said as she gently put the glass down and left.

That was the first and last time she dared to have a drink with them. Though they weren't friendly to her before that drink, no one made an effort after that, not even the secretaries.

She had called one of her friends from college about it, but all John said was, "Fuck 'em if they can't take a joke."

"Thanks, John," she said. "That solves all of my problems."

So, there wasn't a broker with whom she knew she could feel comfortable working on the deal. The choices were slim as it was. The office was divided into specialties. It wasn't like she could ask just any of the brokers. If the base deal worked out, it was a hodgepodge of various specialties: it was an investment deal, an up-fit, an industrial site and a land development all wrapped into one. But the primary deal was an investment deal, her "specialty," and the only other brokers who did investment deals were Bob and Robert. She couldn't stomach working with them, especially Bob. If only he had shown just once that he respected her. But she felt like they were in grade school, and he was always pulling her ponytail in front of all the other boys.

She didn't think too much of Robert, either.

Robert was the top investment broker in a three-state radius, but she didn't like the way he operated. She had endured her share of him when she was his protégé for her first two years in commercial real estate.

"Les, I want you to call that agent on the Oakwood Apartments deal, and tell that residential agent that she's only going to get a quarter of the commission."

"But you already told her the commission was a fifty-fifty split."

"Changed my mind. Besides, it will give you a bigger cut. You'll get $30,000 instead of $10,000.

"Why don't you do it?"

"Because it's good practice for you. Welcome to commercial real estate."

Leslie waited until she got home to call the agent, and when she did, she told her what Robert had said and how awful she felt.

"He can't get away with it," the agent had said.

"Don't count on it. Commercial real estate is a vicious business. If I were you, I'd find a viper of an attorney and let him or her deal with Robert."

That's why the Myrtle Beach deal was going to be her deal until it was sealed. No Robert. No ponytail pulling. No gum. No olives.

She would move more swiftly than the Citadel boys could move.

After making her flight arrangements to D.C., she made some initial contact calls to the companies she would approach if the government meeting turned out well. Out of her list, she was able to speak directly with only one person: a Ron Reilly, who handled acquisitions for Schorr Laboratories in Houston.

Though she didn't tell him where the property was located, or all of the details of space and real estate value, Reilly seemed intrigued. "You called at a good time. We're looking at expanding our operations in the east."

So she booked a flight to Houston for the next week. She would pursue the rest of the companies later. She had a feeling about Schorr Laboratories.

She sat back down at the table and opened up a map of the entire Grand Strand. She traced the miles and townships from the base up to the North Carolina line. She knew she would have to know obscure facts when she met with Reilly. Sometimes companies bought properties based on the total picture: the economy, demographics, tax incentives, and federal money. So she was working on a prospectus for him. Before she would meet with him, she would not only have all of the information memorized, so she could talk about it with ease, but she would have one of the assistants in Charlotte compile it into booklet, presentation form. And with the commercial real estate market in the bottom of a septic tank, she knew that she'd better have it all shining.

As she traced the coastline with her finger, she saw Cherry Grove. She could even tell where the main channel was—the channel that wove with all the other channels for more than two hundred miles of the Intracoastal Waterway. Next to the mouth of the channel, and near her mother's house, she could see Valgooney's island, but she couldn't distinguish where hers ended and Earl's began. The librarian was right. Wherever that line was didn't matter. Both of them owned quite a chunk of land.

That Thursday, after a two-hour flight to D.C. from Myrtle Beach, Leslie sat at a large conference table with three other uniformed men who were all Major This or Captain That. Major Johnson was close to what she had pictured. But she was wrong about his hair: instead of blond wheat, it was black bristles. His personality was like his hair: sharp, with pointed edges. She wondered whether she should have asked one of the Citadel brokers to come with her. They could have done some militaristic back-slapping; but instead, there was nothing to talk about but the deal, and barely that.

There they sat: stiff, corpse-like, staring across the table at her as she explained in nonspecific terms what she thought the "highest and best use" was for the base, and she asked if they would protect her efforts if indeed she brought a willing and able purchaser to them.

When she asked this question, the other officers turned to Johnson, who kept his eyes fixed on her as if she had just asked him if she could borrow a fighter jet for an evening out on the town. He clenched his jaw and then turned to the officer on his right and said, "Gentlemen, why don't we step into the next room for a moment. Excuse us." He stood and the other men followed in a straight line behind him out the door, as if they were going to practice an ROTC formation—the kind she used to watch when she and Andrea would walk around campus when they were in college.

Leslie glanced at her Rolex. Maybe this whole attempt on her part to try to sell the base was ludicrous, and they were in the next room laughing at her. Then they filed back into the room like they had marched out and sat down, simultaneously. Johnson cleared his throat.

"Ms. Ryan, we cannot sign a listing agreement."

Leslie scooted her chair closer to the table. "Major Johnson, I only want someone to sign a form promising that *if* I bring an acceptable offer and it closes, my company will be paid a certain percentage of the deal, that's all. The government is under no obligation other than if we find a buyer, and if, and only if, the offer is acceptable."

"It's not an Exclusive Listing Agreement in any shape or form?"

"No. It's just your basic form. I brought a copy with me." Leslie turned to the chair next to her, where she had set her briefcase. She pulled out a two-page, legal-sized, typed form and slid it across the table. As it slid, fluttering like a trapped moth, Johnson picked it up, and she said, "It's our standard form. If you have any questions about it, call our company attorney in Atlanta. His name and number are on the back."

"I'll have to have our attorneys look it over."

"I understand."

"I'll call you." Johnson stood up.

Leslie pushed her chair back and also stood. The other men remained seated. Maybe they were going to discuss the matter further, she thought. "Do you have any idea when that form will be signed?"

"By the end of next week."

"Thank you for your time." She reached out to shake Johnson's hand, but the other men made no attempt to stand or shake her hand. Johnson didn't walk her to the door, so she turned and nodded a good-bye when she reached the door before leaving.

Sometimes it irked her when men tried the invisible approach—the approach that she thought was intended to make any and all women feel worthless. An invisible approach that meant you weren't there—not in mind, body or soul—unless, she thought, unless they were in the mood to conquer you in bed. Then you weren't invisible. You were a goddamn neon billboard. Or at least their intentions were.

She arrived back in Myrtle at 7:30 p.m. and decided after she changed clothes to walk to Fullwood's Diner and have some greasy food. It was the quickest thing around, although she would have preferred something healthier. It was a real diner, not some new restaurant trying to look old—down to the wide, pink coffee saucers, juke box, swivel bar stools, blowing fans, and one dripping old air conditioning unit, groaning like it was ninety-two years old.

As soon as Leslie opened the screen door into the diner, she was greeted by the same tall, heavy-set man who had waited on her the other day. He was wiping the top of the pink Formica counter. "Just sit anywhere," he said in a thick southern accent. "Be right with you, directly." Then he slung the dingy white rag he had been using to wipe the counter over his shoulder, walked over to the silver coffeemaker, picked up the pot, and walked over to the end of the bar, where a redheaded man with a red beard sat eating a sandwich. "Like I was saying," the man with the beard continued, "My theory is that it's some lazy fisherman that ain't caught nothing all day, so he goes and steals the crabs out of the cage."

The man with the apron poured coffee into the man's saucer. "Maybe you right and all, but this here bandit mostly strikes at night. According to the paper, whoever is responsible, is breaking them traps. They're making sure no crabs gonna get caught again, leastways in that cage. So much for your theory. You sure you don't want another sandwich?"

The man with the beard shook his head and picked up the saucer. From where Leslie was sitting, she could see the coffee slosh from side to side as he moved the saucer to his mouth.

"Be right there, young lady." The man with the apron walked back over to the coffeemaker and set the pot back on the burner. Then he walked to the other end of the bar, where there was an opening, turned sideways and pushed through. It reminded Leslie of the time she watched a pregnant woman try to push through the gate at a New York subway.

He walked over to her table. "Welcome to Fullwood's. I'm Fullwood. Ever been here before?"

"The other day for coffee to go."

"Welcome back. Well, as you can see, ain't nothing fancy, but we sure can make one heck of a burger. Care for a burger?"

"Sounds great. Put everything on it, and I'd like some coffee."

"You got it. And if you want to give this place a little ambiance," —but he said it as "am-be-ants" — "here's some quarters for the jukebox." Fullwood reached into a pocket in his apron and laid three quarters in front of her. "On the house."

"Thank you." Leslie looked around the diner. The jukebox was behind her table, in the corner of the diner closest to the door. The diner had seven wooden tables covered with red-and-white checkered tablecloths. Each table had four high-back chairs. The walls were all wooden, with no windows except for the huge picture window that ran the length of the wall behind the stove and preparation counter. The other counter, where the customer sat, faced directly toward the ocean. Next time, she'd sit there, she thought. She noticed a hallway at the other end of the restaurant—bathrooms, she concluded.

She scooted her chair back and walked over to the jukebox. The quarters clicked as she dropped them into the slot. She ran her right index finger down the glass on the edge of each song title, all of them hits from the forties to the eighties. She punched in the number for Glenn Miller's "When the Swallows Come Back to Capistrano." She ran her finger back up the glass and stopped on an Elvis hit, "Are You Lonely Tonight?" Then she punched in "Love Grows." She turned around, and as the Miller song began to softly play, she heard the bearded man excitedly say:

"Whoever it is, I hope they fry his ass!"

"Watch it, Vince." Fullwood tilted his head in Leslie's direction. "We got us a lady present."

Vince swiveled the stool toward her. "Sorry, ma'am, no offense intended."

"None taken." Leslie turned back toward the jukebox.

"Good selection," Fullwood said, as the Glenn Miller band played.

"Thanks," Leslie said.

Vince nodded in agreement and then swiveled his chair back around as Fullwood bent over and opened what Leslie supposed was a built-in refrigerator. She heard a door shut, and when he stood back up, he had a meat patty in his hand covered in wax paper. He removed the wax paper and slapped the burger on the grill.

"This Crab Bandit is the most exciting thing going on since the Farnsworth fight died down," Fullwood said. He picked up a black spatula and squeezed the burger. It sizzled.

"Speaking of… has you-know-who come back in since all that?" Vince picked up the saucer and gulped. His gulp was so loud that Leslie could hear it.

"No." Without turning to look at Vince, Fullwood flipped the burger over on the grill.

"Lyla seen her at Boulineau's the other day. You know Lyla from the bowling league, don't you?"

"Met her once." Fullwood turned toward Vince.

"Said she was buying herself some red roses, so Lyla says, 'Valgooney, what's a pretty woman like you buying herself flowers for? Men supposed to do that.' Know what she said?"

Fullwood shook his head and turned to flip the burger again.

"Said, 'Where is that written?' Lyla didn't know what to think, so she just walked away."

Fullwood turned in his direction. "So?"

"Come on. A woman buying herself flowers?"

"Heck, if they was to wait on us to buy them flowers, every florist on the Strand would be out of business."

"I'm just telling you what I heard. Know what else? Time before that Lyla saw her at the store stocking up on a bunch of rice, I mean like fifty-five pounds, and a pile of vegetables and some of that tofu—you know that stuff that looks like fatback floating in water? So Lyla asks why she don't have any meat in her cart. Know what she said?"

Fullwood twisted the red tie off of a plastic bag of buns, took one out and set it on the counter. "Sounds like it's going to be a mystery." He opened the refrigerator and pulled out a plastic container of mayonnaise and set it on the counter next to the bun.

"Said she was one of them vegetarians. Now they are some weird people, them vegetarians. Vegetarians. Just sounds weird. It ain't American." Vince shook his head and made the stool swivel.

Fullwood began spreading the mayonnaise on the bun.

"I'm serious, Fullwood. Something ain't right. Been hiding out on that island since her parents died. Don't eat meat."

"Ain't against the law to be different."

"Maybe it ain't, but it just ain't American."

"Boy, I'm sure you didn't make no 'A' in history."

"What's that supposed to mean?" Vince asked.

Fullwood put a tomato slice, cheese, chopped onions, slaw, and pickles on top of the burger, and then the bun. "Nothing," he said to Vince, and then he turned in Leslie's direction. "Ma'am?"

Leslie looked across the diner at Fullwood.

"Cream and sugar with your coffee?" She had been sitting at the table looking at the checkered tablecloth, hoping they thought she was absorbed in her thoughts and not listening to them. In fact, she had barely even heard the Miller song. Maybe that's what ants felt like at picnics: busy but trying to stay anonymous.

"Yes, cream and sugar." And she wanted to add, "Please keep talking." The more she heard about Valgooney, the more she wanted to know. But why would Valgooney want to talk to her? This wasn't college. This was adulthood, when you had to earn your friendships—at least the ones worth having. She heard the jukebox click, and "Are You Lonely Tonight?" began playing. Funny, Leslie thought, because even though she chose the song, she had not chosen her loneliness.

THE DEAL

"I like the specs and the numbers, and especially the location. You know if we do this deal, we'll transfer at least a hundred folks from here and hire about three hundred there," Ron Reilly said as he continued flipping through the prospectus that Leslie had managed to compile before her flight out of Charlotte. Susan, the office assistant, had a knack for making things look professional within hours of receiving the information. And in this case, it had only been three days since Leslie had met with Major Johnson, and now she was in Houston.

"Our transferees will love being right on the ocean." As he said this, he ran his index and middle fingers over the thick brown mustache that jutted beyond the confines of his mouth. "We'll have to make sure there aren't any young things sunbathing nearby, or we might have a chemical mishap, mix the wrong solutions," and he laughed, running his fingers over his mustache again.

Leslie wondered why he kept fingering his mustache. Most body language was simple, but his finger-fondling didn't seem like a contemplative dance, or nervousness.

"I know the Chamber of Commerce will be pleased to hear about the number of jobs it's going to create," she said. "Maybe the mayor will present Schorr with keys to the city."

"Actually," Reilly began but stopped. "I'd rather not have any press about this thing until the deal closes. Nobody needs to know anything about it until we've completed our renovations and moved there, if you know what I mean."

Leslie nodded, but she wasn't quite sure what he meant, because most companies wanted the accolades, and whatever kind of tax deal they could make with the county and the state. "What is your time frame as far as taking this a step further?"

Reilly leaned back in his leather chair a little too far, almost knocking into a table behind him. He put his hands behind his head as if to compensate, his mustache-fondling on hold. "My guess is that I could have a decision in a week." Then he moved his chair forward. She heard his feet plop on the carpet. He clasped his hands on top of the desk. "I don't like wasting anybody's time, especially mine, so we could close in, say, ninety days after a thirty-day due diligence."

Leslie sat in front of Reilly, separated from him by his large, tidy, gray contemporary desk, trying not to think about how much commission she would earn. Her rough estimate was that after Havelock got its share, hers would be at least $200,000. But she promised herself that she would stay focused on doing a good job and taking the deal to the table. Her mother used to say that when an agent focused only on the commission, then that agent might as well kiss that deal good-bye. Leslie had heard this so many times that she could quote her: "…because if you become too focused on the money, you end up not giving a squat about the customer." Service, she always said, had to be the focus. And then she would add, "Besides, agents are their own worst competition." So Leslie tried not to think about the commission, even though she hadn't earned any money in two years, not since the market crashed, compliments of a perfect financial storm. Instead, she had blown through CD's, insurance policies, and all of her savings. Her debt-to-income ratio would make a mortgage broker hyperventilate.

Leslie's mother could outshine Suze Orman, while Leslie's financial situation was the Glenn Beck of debt: loud, ludicrous, and no resolution in sight—unless that is, this deal closed. It might not wipe out all of her debt, but at least she could breathe again. So not craving the deal to close was as challenging as the transaction itself.

Leslie nodded to Reilly's comment about the due diligence and the potential closing date, and said, "All I need is a week's notice to arrange it with my contact in Washington. They call it 'clearance.' Just so you are forewarned, you must have a letter of intent and at least a $50,000 binder before they will let you step onto the premises."

"Is that binder refundable, or is Uncle Sam looking to collect on the initial look-see?" Reilly moved his hands back behind his head again.

"It's refundable for the first view, but then you'll have to put up some at-risk money for the due diligence."

"How much for the due diligence?"

"I would suggest an additional $50,000 to show that your company is serious."

"Typical," Reilly said. "Well then, Leslie, you may have just saved me months of poring over deals that make no sense. Because, if every thing is as good as your prospectus claims, we might just have a deal. Care to do a little celebrating? I could show you some great night spots."

"Thanks. I only flew in for the day. I've been out of town so much lately, working on this deal, that for all I know, my office manager has sublet my desk."

He moved his hands from behind his head ran his fingers back over his mustache again. Leslie noticed he was wearing a thin gold band on his left hand, and that after he finished fondling his mustache, he twisted his ring around a couple of times.

"The least I could do is show you around the facility. It might help you to see how the military base suits us as your prospectus indicates." He raised his thick eyebrows. Leslie thought his eyebrows were cloned twins. She wondered if he would begin fondling those.

"I think that would be helpful." She uncrossed her legs and started to stand up. As she stood, she smoothed down her the front of her skirt.

He walked over to the door and took his suit jacket, hanging on a hook behind the door, and put it on over his white starched shirt. He turned the door handle and opened the door. "Let's go down to the lab."

Leslie pulled her purse strap over her shoulder and reached for her briefcase.

"You're welcome to leave it here. No one will touch it, I promise." He stood in the doorway, but he didn't move from the doorway until she was close to it. Then he turned to the side and let her pass, going first. "Turn right. We'll take the elevator at the end of the hall."

The hallway was long, like a lane in a bowling alley, without windows or other doors to offices. The light gray carpet made the hallway seem two-dimensional, she thought.

While they were waiting for the elevator door to open, she turned to look at Reilly. "How long have you been with Schorr Laboratories?"

"Since day one, twenty-five years ago. That's how long we've been in business. You might say that I'm one of the founders."

She should have known that, she thought to herself. That's what she got for getting caught up in the moment of the deal. Details, she thought to herself, those damn details. At least he didn't seem to mind that she hadn't known this detail, so she decided to ignore her faux pas.

The elevator doors opened, and they rattled as it moved in the frame.

Reilly and Leslie stepped inside. Reilly pressed the "L" key. The doors shut.

When the doors rattled opened again, he said, "Here we are." He waited for her to walk past him. "Turn to the left."

Leslie stepped off of the elevator and into another long hallway. Unlike the floor above, a window ran the length of the entire floor. As she began walking down the hallway, she could feel him walking close behind. She never liked it when anyone invaded her space...*my space*, she thought, and the phrase seemed like an oxymoron, since so many things were now public domain.

"Look through the windows," he said.

She stopped. She saw a large lab with at least twenty people wearing lab jackets, working at various tables.

"This is what we call the nucleus of our entire operation. The scientists you see were recruited from the best schools in the country."

"What are they working on?"

"The structure of brain tissue and embryos."

She noticed one of the female scientists, who sat peering intently into a microscope. Romanesque, she thought. The woman had a Romanesque nose. "Embryos?"

She felt Reilly looking at her.

"It's part of the reason we want to expand our company in Myrtle."

"For your patent on antidepressants?"

"Antidepressants?" She watched him finger his mustache.

"I thought that's why you needed more space."

"No. This new thing is going to make the chill pill seem like Kool-Aid." He began fingering his mustache again.

She was feeling stupid. Why hadn't she researched more on Schorr on the Internet?

"The gene," he said. "The gay gene. That's why we're expanding."

"To explore it?" She asked it as a question, but she wished it had come out like a statement, so that she could feel some semblance of knowledge and control again, especially since she had already screwed up.

Reilly laughed. When he did, his mustache bounced, like it was on a trampoline.

"Guess you're too busy brokering deals to keep up with the latest scientific quandaries. Not that someone with your good looks would keep up with the ongoing gay issue." He smiled and said, "We've already explored the gay gene. We've isolated it. The next step is to destroy it. Decimate it. Can you imagine? No more male hairdressers, naughty Catholic priests, florists, dykes, or your basic pedophile, cruising the public parks, preying on children. And to think we can take care of all of that in the embryo. Incredible isn't it?"

Leslie swallowed hard, but she couldn't look at him, so instead she looked down at the floor. "Don't you think the activists are going to fight?" She asked this as she raised her eyes from the floor to his.

He ran his fingers over his mustache again. "Maybe, but it's going to be extremely difficult to do when the APA reverses its ruling."

"The APA?"

"My dear, the American Psychological Association. That's the organization that decides what's normal or not. Guess what's going back on the list?"

"They can do that?"

"With some prodding and some religious alliances." He laughed. "This is the only arena where science is a good friend of religion." Then he laughed again.

Just what was so damn funny, she wanted to ask. She wanted to yank his mustache off of his face and stomp on it like a bug. Instead, she looked into the lab.

"When we first discovered the gene, all of the networks were swarming around this place. The Christians were worried that our discovery would give gays rights. I got calls from every gay organization throughout the United States. Guess they should be worried."

Leslie thought that "proof" was a joke because what really had a guarantee or warranty? Reilly was still babbling on.

"But now," he said, "since we can pinpoint it to sweet momma's womb, there's no telling what's gonna happen next."

"Does anyone really win?" she asked. As she said "win," she felt sick, like she did the night her mother made the announcement about selling the company: the kind of sickness when you know that you're on your own ground zero.

"We win," Reilly said. He looked at her with his hairy eyebrows raised, as if she should have gotten this too.

She glanced at her watch. "Mr. Reilly, I suppose I should leave for the airport."

"Sure, but you better call me 'Ron.'" He used his thumb to point toward the elevator, like he was going to hitchhike. "Do you need a cab?"

"Yes."

"I'll call one for you from the lobby."

"I need to get my briefcase."

"Right. Then, I'll call for one from my office." He turned around and began walking toward the elevator.

"Ron? Is there a ladies' room in the lobby? If so, if you don't mind, could you bring the briefcase down?"

He turned his head slightly over his shoulder. "Sure. No problem. You feel all right?"

"I'm fine. Just worried I'll miss my flight," she said in her telephone voice. *Yeah, I'm just fine,* she thought. "Fine" as when she went in for a mammogram and loved it; "fine" as irritable bowel syndrome; "fine" as how much she'd like to scream "FUCK YOU, you mustached, homophobic prick!"

As Reilly turned his head back around, Leslie quickly rubbed the back of her hand over her forehead. Anger, she thought, can eat at you like some cannibal, and your only defense was to eat it back. And "letting go," she thought, was a bunch of psychological bullshit. They have it all wrong. You've got to eat it. That's the only thing anger understands. Eat it harder and faster than it can eat you.

Before she boarded the plane, she checked her voice mail. Reilly had already called. "Remember, don't say *anything* about what we discussed today. I don't like putting out any fires unless I have to, okay? Okay." Leslie could have sworn that she heard his mustache brush against the phone before he hung up. Blake had also left a message: "The commission agreement was faxed to us this morning. I'm very proud of you, but make sure there's not an asbestos problem this time." Even when he was attempting to be supportive, Leslie couldn't help but feel irritated because he didn't know how to. His compliments were a "Catch-22." Maybe she shouldn't fault him. Maybe his parents never instilled in him some basic human skills. But could you? Could you instill humanity? Or install it? It's not like it's some product that you could buy at Home Depot. Is it ever the parents' fault? Maybe they tried, but Blake was humanity-challenged. That was probably the nicest thing he had said to her in a year. This was the deal that would earn her the respect she wanted at Havelock. And her own respect as well.

ANDREA

Leslie sat next to the window on the flight back to Charlotte. As the flight attendants finished their emergency procedures speech and the plane began taxiing down the runway, she leaned against the window. A few minutes later, she stared down onto the miles of land below that, from where she was sitting, looked perfectly divided.

She looked at the panel above her. She could tell they still hadn't reached altitude, because the seat belt light was on. She always felt anxious during this part because it made her feel like everybody on the plane was in an unspoken danger zone that would end as soon as the light flashed off. That was a lot of power for such a little light, she thought. She had felt this way long before 9/11, and that horrible incident had only increased her trepidation. She peered out the window again.

She had only been to Texas one other time—a college graduation present to herself after answering the switchboard every weekend for a year at one of her mother's offices.

She and Andrea had left Charlotte to spend a month driving out west. They didn't have a destination or a plan—

only to go wherever the mood took them, promising to check in every few days with their parents.

She closed her eyes. Every once in a while, she could go an entire day without some reminder of her, like the wall mural in the living room in Charlotte that Andrea painted the year after that trip out west. It was a combination of a self-portrait of Andrea on one side of a huge shimmering mountain, and an abstract of Leslie on the other side of it, joined together by a thin dark blue streak of light emanating from one eye to another. Andrea always explained to those who commented on it, "It's Superman's beam. Penetrates just like him. It's all in the eyes, you know." Sometimes Leslie would lie on the hardwood floor in front of the painting, flipping through mental snapshots of Andrea. She would close her eyes, as she was doing now, and see those extra-long eyelashes that looked like some awning over a building, hovering over her light brown eyes, and her curly brown waist-long hair.

Everything was long about Andrea. Long legs, even though she was only five-foot-six; and how she loved to wear long dresses. In the late eighties, even when tie-dye hadn't yet made its way back into fashion, that's what Andrea wore: long tie-dye dresses, mostly of her own creation. She was "going to paint the world in tie-dye one day," her answer to those people who would ask her what she was going to do with a degree in art. "No, really," they would say in response. "Really," she'd repeat. "I'm going to paint the world in tie-dye, and I'm going to work with junior high school kids, so they won't be as pinched as us when they grow up."

Leslie and Andrea had met in a political science class during July of 1993, at the University of North Carolina-Charlotte, when they were rising seniors, trying to knock out some electives. It was a class on Latin American politics, and the University had hired a visiting Latin American specialist.

The class was full for a political science class: at least thirty-five students, all complacent except for Andrea, who sat on the far left row (not because of the professor, but because it was summer), next to the window; and a guy with short blond hair whose uniform was khakis and a different-colored button-down shirt every day, five days a week for five and a half weeks. He looked like a Nazi-Aryan, she thought. He sat in the middle of the room, but on the first row, close enough to make Leslie wonder whether he was trying to kiss the professor's ass or to control both sides of the room. Leslie sat against the far right wall, next to the door and under the pencil sharpener.

She didn't notice Andrea until the fifth day of class: the day Andrea and the blond guy got into it. The class was supposed to have read Castro's treatise, "History Will Absolve Me"; only it seemed like no one had read it except for Andrea, Leslie, and the blond guy.

The blond guy said, "We should just invade and control the governments of Cuba, El Salvador, and anywhere else there's a problem with freedom, because if we don't, they'll all be communists. All the communists want to do is take over the world, rule it their way!"

Leslie noticed how his face had turned slightly red when he finished speaking. It contrasted with his blond hair.

The professor paced across the front of the room near the chalk board. "Anyone care to respond to his comment?"

"I do," Andrea said. She turned to the blond guy. "Could you explain to me how the United States would be acting any differently, if we invade these countries, than what you're accusing the communists of doing?" She flipped her hair, which was hanging down her front, to the back. Her face was totally blank: no raised eyebrows or curl of the lip, just her eyelashes that jutted out. Even those were still. No blink.

Leslie looked from Andrea to the blond guy, whose face was redder than before. "Sure, because we're the United

Julie E. Townsend

States!" And as he said "the United States," Leslie saw some spit flying out of the side of his mouth. He reminded her of a race horse, pushed to the maximum.

"And that gives us the right to rule and dominate the world?" Andrea asked, still calm, still blank.

The blond guy turned around so quickly in his chair that his desk rocked. Leslie fantasized him toppling over. He pointed his finger at Andrea, shouting, "IT'S PEOPLE LIKE YOU THAT'S SCREWED UP AMERICA!"

"Now there's a logical reason to infringe on another country's sovereignty," Andrea said.

Leslie was amazed at her calm, especially since she suddenly felt nervous.

The professor, who had been pacing in front of the room, up to the point when the blond guy almost tipped over his desk, suddenly stopped as if he weren't allowed to move one step further in any direction. He abruptly changed the subject.

Now they were going to talk about Batista.

Andrea looked at Leslie, raised her eyebrows, and tilted her head slightly in the direction of the blond guy, as if to say, "Can you believe this guy?"

The blond guy looked at the professor as he repositioned himself back in his seat. His face wasn't as red.

Leslie turned to scan the room. The students, who hadn't moved for the last few class sessions, were all sitting up; a few even had their mouths open, as if they were trying to decide whether it was safe to take a nap again. Despite their complacency, Leslie remembered how the energy of the class remained tense for the remaining weeks of the summer session. It reminded her of why her mother had divorced her father: There was always a brewing argument, ready to blow at his whim. The trouble was, his whims were unpredictable: She never knew what would set him off. Would it be because her mother didn't fix a recipe just like his mother did when he was a child? Or that Leslie didn't put the fork on the correct side of the plate? Was he going to accuse her mother of cheating on him, again, when she was only out showing houses?

After class, Leslie followed Andrea out into the hallway and told her she had agreed with her. Andrea called him "a militaristic prick."

"I'm sorry I didn't jump into the debate, but it didn't look like you needed any help."

"I don't think his male ego could have taken on another female."

They both laughed.

Since neither one had a boyfriend—Leslie had broken up with Tom just a few weeks before summer school began, and Andrea had not had a steady boyfriend in four months—they began to do everything together.

Less than a year later, they took the graduation trip that Andrea called "the paint on the canvas of our friendship."

Leslie's head bumped against the airplane window. She opened her eyes. "Sorry, folks," the pilot said over the intercom, "we're going to experience a little turbulence for a while. Strong headwinds." Leslie looked out the window. She could see for miles, so they weren't going to crash and die, she thought, as she closed her eyes again.

She saw Andrea stretched out on a pile of rocks fifty feet from the shore of a lake, surrounded by snow-capped Montana mountains. The locals called it "Diamond Head Rock." It was thirty feet of boulders all clumped together, some boulders larger than the others, with one of the largest boulders jutting straight up, with one smooth side.

They had discovered Diamond Head after renting a cabin in Ennis, Montana, a tiny town they found after leaving Texas, Colorado, and Wyoming, driving aimlessly through the countryside. It's where they decided to stay for the remaining three weeks of their vacation.

The entire house was no larger than Leslie's bedroom at home. From the outside, it looked like an enlarged doll house: white with a pale green trim. Inside, all packed into one room, with the exception of the bathroom, there was a double bed pushed up against one of the walls, a clothes rack, one dresser, a small wooden table with two folding metal chairs, a miniature stove, a refrigerator and a single sink.

The closest town, only slightly larger than Ennis and fourteen miles away, looked like something out of a western movie, with its wooden sidewalks and swinging doors to the only bar in town. But it did have a Dairy Queen and a small grocery store. "This is doing America," Andrea had said. "And it's cheap."

Almost every day, they would pack books, sandwiches, and beer, and walk two miles down a narrow dirt road to Diamond Head Rock.

It became a ritual: Once they were at the edge of the lake, Andrea took off her shoes and left them beside a small bush. She hoisted the backpack off of her shoulder and held it above her head. Leslie would do the same as they waded out to the rocks in their bathing suits.

The first time they discovered the rocks, Leslie was hesitant.

"What if there are rattlesnakes living on the rocks?"

"I'll beat them with a book."

They began walking into the water. When they reached the rocks, the water was up to their necks. They tossed their backpacks on the rocks and grabbed onto a small jagged edge and hoisted themselves up.

They would lie stretched out on the rocks like lizards in the sun, surrounded by snow-capped mountains. Hundred-degree heat with no humidity, not like Charlotte in the summer.

Leslie raised her head to see a boat she heard in the distance. As she did, she looked at Andrea, who was lying near her. Though she had always thought Andrea was attractive, she had never noticed how beautiful she was until that moment; she felt uncomfortable for thinking so.

That evening, when they sat on a ridge near the cabin watching the sun set, it was the brightest orange Leslie had ever seen, giving everything an orange tint: her arms, Andrea's face and hair. She felt uncomfortable again because she wanted to stroke Andrea's orange sun-setting hair.

Why was she thinking these things? She had dated Tom all during college. He was thoughtful, and the sex was good. The only reason she ended it was because they were growing apart. And just what did that mean, she had wondered: "Growing apart"? You didn't talk anymore? You didn't turn each other on like you used to? Were relationships supposed to be one constant forward movement on some path she never could find? Her parents' rocky relationship was no lesson in love. How would she know how to resolve a conflict when her parents could only respond to a conflict?

When her mother began dating again after the divorce, Leslie realized that her business-savvy mother was an utter failure in her choices of men. Was her mother that insecure despite the enormous success of her business? How could her mother soar as the CEO of a multimillion-dollar business, teach others how to be successful in sales, and be a guest speaker for countless businesses all over the country, but date men who were obvious losers, from the top of their toupee heads down to their outdated polyester suits? Maybe the losers were the only men who weren't intimidated by her mother's success because they were too stupid to know any better, or maybe they saw her as a way out of Loserville.

So Leslie had no clue what made a good relationship; she only knew when it was time to dump it in the landfill and let it rot properly. Why couldn't she have a relationship with a man that mirrored her ever-growing friendship with Andrea? They called each other on the phone several times a day, and no matter what mood Andrea was in, or what

Julie E. Townsend

she needed to do, it wasn't an intrusion. It was always an enhancement of her day in ways that she couldn't describe. She should have felt this way about Tom or the guys she had dated before him.

Andrea shifted her legs as they watched the sun set, and when she did, her left knee rested against Leslie's knee, which was also crossed, jutting out. Leslie slowly moved her knee away from Andrea's. She didn't want to; she had to.

Maybe if she thought about when she last had sex with Tom, it would help. But it wouldn't, because what she felt toward Andrea wasn't sexual; all she wanted was to somehow never let go of the emotion; an emotion that made her earlier crushes seem like preschool.

"There's some strange vibes coming from the west of me. Care to share your canyon?" Andrea had asked.

Leslie shook her head.

"I'll be back in a few minutes." Andrea uncrossed her legs, stood up and walked down the ridge across the road from the cabin. As soon as Leslie saw her go into the tiny house, she slapped her forehead and said to herself, "Get a grip. She's your best friend, dammit."

She looked down between her legs at the patch of earth jutting out from where she sat, and she began picking up small rocks and sheaves of grass and flinging them away from her.

She heard a door slam and looked toward the dollhouse. Andrea was crossing the road and had something in her hand, but Leslie didn't want to stare. She played with the dirt, trying not to think that any moment Andrea would sit back down beside her.

"Look what I've got." Andrea plopped down on the grass next to her and held out a fifth of Tequila, Cuervo Gold.

"Where have you been hiding it?" Leslie stole a quick look at her but then averted her eyes to her tennis shoes.

"Where isn't as important as why." Andrea twisted the cap off the bottle. Leslie heard the paper seal tear.

"Why?" Leslie said, but she still didn't look at her.

"Because when I wasn't paying attention, somebody—and I'm not naming names—built a goddamn wall between us, and if it takes a little cacti nectar to climb the wall, then maybe we won't care about any bruises." Andrea tilted the bottle toward Leslie and took a gulp. After she swallowed, she said, "Sweet communion for Jesus! If my throat lining and intestines live to tell the story, I might forget that you're holding out on me." As she handed Leslie the bottle, the tequila swished inside the bottle, like a wave washing in, instead of washing something away.

As Leslie lifted the bottle up toward her lips and began tilting her head backward, Andrea said, "Hold on. You've got to make a toast."

Leslie looked at her. "But you didn't."

"I brought the bottle. According to the rules, I'm excused."

"What rules?"

"Exactly."

Leslie shook her head and then focused on a small rock a few feet away from her as she tilted the bottle toward Andrea. "To one's own truth, even if no one understands it, including oneself."

Looking away from Andrea, she took a long swig.

Leslie started to hand her the bottle, but Andrea lifted her hand and waved her a "no."

"Go ahead," she said. "I think you need to have several swigs until I don't feel the wall anymore."

"Trying to get me drunk?"

"Whatever it takes."

Leslie leaned her head back and took another gulp. She could feel it burn from her tongue and down into her stomach, but she knew she wouldn't be able to drink away what she felt, not like she did the first time she had sex.

"Here," she said as she abruptly handed Andrea the bottle.

Andrea took the bottle from her, took a swig and looked over at Leslie.

"Don't look at me." Leslie's voice quivered slightly when she said this. She breathed in deeply, so deeply that she almost took away her own breath. "Maybe I do need one more swig."

Andrea handed her the bottle, and the liquor swished.

This time, Leslie took several gulps. The tequila burned; she could feel her fear being lulled into a nap, a cat's nap. The kind of nap that, when you wake it, the cat looks as if it has been dreaming for a hundred years. She handed the bottle back to Andrea. "You know I really liked Tom, don't you?"

She nodded.

"He was the best boyfriend I've ever had, but...but I'm afraid that you won't be my friend anymore once I tell you. I just hope that you will still be my best friend, no matter what." Leslie felt her eyes well up with tears, and they began rolling down her face. Before she could wipe her eyes, she felt Andrea's fingers stopping the flow on the right side of her face.

Leslie looked at her wet fingers.

"I forgot the salt," Andrea said.

Leslie smiled.

"So what is it? I know. You really wanted to break up with Tom just to go out with that Nazi from our Poli Sci class last summer?"

Leslie smiled. "Don't try to make me laugh right now when I'm scared, because I wish that I could have what we have in our friendship, in a relationship. It makes me feel lonely thinking I'll never have that without you." She buried her head in her upright knees. "I only hope that you'll still be my friend."

Andrea wrapped her arm around Leslie's shoulders and held her tightly as she whispered, "I'm flattered that you want what we have in our friendship. I do know what you mean, but I've never thought about playing tennis on the other side of the court."

Leslie kept her head buried in her knees. "Me either. I wouldn't know how to make that serve. That's why I'm so freaked out. And I wouldn't have said anything except that you got me drunk."

"That's why you're my heroine for saying what you did. And don't worry. Your secret is safe with me. I won't tell the guy at the Dairy Queen down the road that you really want me, not him."

Leslie looked at her, "You're an asshole."

"Now that's classy. Is that how you come onto women?"

Leslie laughed. "All the time, as you know." Leslie picked up the bottle of tequila and handed it to Andrea. "Now it's your turn to get drunk."

"Why, so you can take advantage of me?"

"So that's how this is going to go for the rest of the vacation? All of a sudden I'm gay and you get to crack jokes about me?"

Andrea smiled and took a swig, as she reassured Leslie that their friendship was still intact, even though neither one said much for almost two days.

Night time was the most awkward, especially that night, because when they finally knew they needed to sleep, both tired and drunk, Leslie worried that she would accidentally roll over while she was sleeping and touch her.

In the middle of the night, Leslie woke up suddenly, dreaming that she had touched her face, as softly as Andrea had touched her tears. When she realized she had only been dreaming, she turned slowly to see how far away she was from Andrea's side of the bed. Andrea was lying flat on her back, soundly sleeping, with those long eyelashes pointed up toward the ceiling. Leslie scooted as far away as she could, almost falling off of the bed.

Three days later—the day before they were to begin the trip back home—they packed their last lunch to Diamond Head Rock and stretched out in their usual positions.

Without warning, Andrea moved closer toward her and wedged her hand into Leslie's. As soon as Andrea touched her, Leslie jerked. She remembered thinking Tom's hand never felt so soft.

Andrea, still holding her hand, looked at her and said, "I'm glad you told me first. I was beginning to think maybe I was the weird one. But when I got you to confess that you have more feelings for me than just a friend, I didn't know what to say, just like you didn't. Isn't it strange? You read about this stuff, hear about it, and then it happens to you and it makes you question everything you've ever thought about the way things are supposed to be, at least how they say things are 'supposed to be.'"

"So what are we going to do about it?" Leslie asked.

"Do about it? You don't waste any time, do you?"

"Always joking up an awkward moment, aren't you?" Leslie said.

"We do whatever, wherever, our feelings take us. I think that's how we got to this point in the first place."

Later that night, as they lay in the bed in that tiny dollhouse of a house, they discussed how they had to keep things quiet. They had already heard a couple of horror stories from college. One young woman Andrea knew had tried to commit suicide after her parents kicked her out of the house, when she confessed she was in love with a woman. Leslie had heard of a guy whose parents always acted as if their son had some disease whenever they talked about him. How could one's parents emotionally kill off their own?

They never guessed then that these stories were just the beginning of their own collection: real stories that made fiction seem as watered-down as a cheap drink; stories that began with a feeling that Leslie could never explain well.

No wonder homosexuality was the big bogeyman. If *they* couldn't explain it, how could anyone else understand?

Andrea asked, "How do you say to someone, 'I know what a cloud feels like'?"

"What are you talking about?" Leslie asked as she rolled onto her side, naked, facing Andrea, who lay on her back looking at the ceiling.

"Making love with you."

"A cloud? Does that mean I'm fluffy? Not firm? Dark and brooding?"

Andrea rolled onto her side, looking at Leslie. "I'm talking esoteric here. Your touch, my touch. How in a weird sort of way, it's like touching yourself."

"That's called masturbation, not clouds." Leslie said.

She laughed. "I'm talking about the softness."

"Okay, how about cotton balls, then?"

A s they left Montana, Andrea and Leslie decided they didn't want any parental pressure, so they wouldn't say anything. They would pretend to be the good friends they had been. Before the Kansas state line, they were still pondering what was so evil, so horrible, about how they felt about each other.

As they crossed into Kansas, Andrea told her that she loved her. "Are you afraid if you say it, then you instantly become a lesbian?"

"Maybe."

"Sweetheart, let the labels begin, because the labels don't make you; you make the labels."

"Okay. I love you, too, dammit. Is that better?"

"Romantic, especially with the 'dammit.'"

On I-70, still in Kansas, Andrea flipped through the buttons on the car radio. She stopped when she heard some preacher screaming, "AND GOD SAID! HELL IS FOR THOSE FORNICATORS, RAPISTS, MURDERERS, PERVERTS AND HOMOSEXUALS!"

"Turn it off," Leslie demanded, as she kept both hands on the steering wheel.

"Fine company we keep. Wonder how long it took that preacher to lump all of those people together? How are we comparable to 'PERVERTS, RAPISTS AND MURDERS'?" Andrea said, mimicking the preacher. "I can see the fornicator part because we aren't married, but that's their fault. They won't let people who love and care about each other marry, so I guess we're fornicating homosexuals. Sounds like all we do all day is stay in bed. Wish we had the time, don't you?" Andrea leaned over to Leslie and kissed her on the corner of her mouth.

That was another thing Leslie had not anticipated—how soft a woman's skin felt. Even when Tom had shaved thirty minutes before their dates, his skin never felt as soft as Andrea's. It had amazed Andrea too. "I'm going to paint this one day."

"My skin?"

"Your kiss, in abstract."

When Leslie heard the attendant's cart rattle, coming closer to her aisle, she opened her eyes.

"What may I get for you?" he asked.

"Red wine, please."

"Seven dollars," he said.

He handed her a small green bottle of wine with a plastic cup turned upside-down on top of the bottle. She gave him a ten-dollar bill and told him to keep the change.

She moved the lever to the pull-down tray in front of her, twisted off the cap to the bottle and poured the wine into the cup. She took a sip and looked out the window. It looked like they were flying somewhere over New Orleans because she could see the Gulf and a huge city that seemed to take the plane a few minutes to fly over. "Sin City," she thought.

She thought again about the preacher on the radio that day in Kansas, and how sometimes Andrea would beg Leslie to watch Jimmy Swaggart's show with her. Leslie had to admit how funny it was when he got upset—tears streaming down his face—crying over the sins of the world; the same sins that they had heard on the radio that day in Kansas.

She also thought it was ironic when Swaggart's ministry was eventually defamed because of his proclivity for prostitutes.

She had wished, when his "sins" were the headlines, that Andrea could have been there to laugh with her. She knew Andrea would have laughed her ass off. But she had already been dead a year when Swaggart fell.

They had lived together for almost nine years when Andrea's pain began almost as quickly as her life ended. One week they were sharing their lives together—Andrea teaching, painting, and Leslie selling enough homes that they had already bought one together. But the next week, she was diagnosed with ovarian cancer that rapidly spread into her other organs.

The day of the funeral was when Leslie told her mother about her "real" life. Though her mother was of some comfort that day, the weeks and months that followed were the beginning of what Leslie often referred to as "the Inquisition." Her mother said, "She just didn't look like one of those, well, you know, dykes. And neither do you. You know you could have any man you want. You're smart, attractive, successful; and one day, you're going to own the company." Other times she would seem angry, as if she were trying to find a home for the blame: "Was it something I did or didn't do?" And she always added, "You know, if you continue this lifestyle, it could hurt your career. People hate queers."

She felt the plane jolt again. It caused the wine in the plastic cup to slosh over onto the built-in tray. She didn't care. She watched it roll off the side of the tray. Leslie picked up the cup and took another sip. "Yes, mother," she thought. "People hate queers because what people don't understand, they want to decimate."

She thought about the time, a year after Andrea died, when her mother asked her if she ever went out to the "queer" bars, and just what did people do in there anyway? Leslie told her that she had not been in years. "It wasn't our venue," she said. Her mother had only shaken her head and asked, "Did you see any of those transvestite people? You know, men dressing up like women and women who want to be men? I just don't understand how you could hang out with such sick trash!" As her mother reached inside a kitchen cabinet for a juice glass, she slammed the door shut.

"Mother, a gay person doesn't want to be another sex— they want the same sex—get it?"

"I just don't understand it. Do you have gay friends? Is that Sally woman, well, you know, a lesbian?"

"Ask her, if you're so curious."

"Well, do you?" Her mother stood with her hands on her hips. "Do you have gay friends?"

"We had some friends who happened to be gay, but mostly Andrea and I did our own thing, had our own life."

Her mother had only shaken her head and said, "I hope to God no one in the family ever hears about it."

Leslie looked around the plane. The woman in front of her was bent over talking to her child. She couldn't hear what she was saying, but the child was giggling. She took another sip of wine and looked at her watch. Another hour and a half at least, back to Charlotte and to the house she had shared with Andrea. Tomorrow, she would drive back to Myrtle and closer to the deal: the deal that began with a creative thought and an assertive push. She wondered what Andrea would have thought about her making a lot of money from other people's prejudices.

WORLD WAR III

"Morton's has the best lobster, you know," Leslie's mother said as she took the cloth napkin from the middle of her plate and shook it lightly, so that it unfolded automatically as she laid it in her lap.

"I didn't know that," Leslie said. She closed the menu and held it propped upright in her lap, and then leaned closer to the table so she could see what assortment of bread was in the cloth-lined basket. "Looks like whole wheat rolls. Care for one?"

"They also have the best Caesar salads around. You should get a Caesar salad and the lobster." Her mother looked over at the hostesses' stand. She leaned toward Leslie. "Don't look, but there's the Myrtle Beach mayor and his new wife. She's rather young to be his wife, don't you think?"

Leslie didn't move her eyes away from her mother's face. "Since you won't let me look, I couldn't tell you."

"You can look now." Leslie eyes followed in the direction of her mother's head.

"What do you think?" Her mother asked as she turned back around.

"I can't say. I could only see his bald spot and her butt."

"Have you ladies decided on a wine yet?" The waiter asked as he approached the table.

"Could you recommend something?" Leslie asked.

"We have an excellent house Fumé. Shall I bring you a glass, or would you prefer a bottle?" He put his hands behind his back.

"Mother? Shall we be decadent and go with a bottle?"

Her mother said, "It's your decision." She turned to the waiter. "My daughter is treating me to dinner."

The waiter, with his hands still behind his back, smiled at Leslie. "A birthday?"

Leslie shook her head sideways and said, "We'll have a bottle."

The waiter turned around, dropped his hands to his sides and walked to the bar near the entrance of the restaurant.

Leslie took a roll out of the basket and put it on her bread plate.

"So everything went as expected in Houston?"

"Sort of." Leslie took a small bite and swallowed hard.

"They *are* going to close on it, aren't they?" Her mother raised her tapered eyebrows.

"It's scheduled around the beginning of November. They have some due diligence to complete to make sure that it fits in with their research development."

"Make sure you talk to my accountant when it does. That's an awful large commission not to have any guidance."

"Ladies?" the waiter asked. He had already uncorked the bottle, and it was in an ice bucket with a towel wrapped around it. He poured the wine halfway into each glass and put the bottle back in the bucket. "I'll be back to take your order in just a few minutes."

"What kind of research do they do?" her mother asked.

"Antidepressants." Leslie took a sip of the wine. The cool swallow warmed her and gave her an instant shot of liquid bravery. She decided to add, "They also discovered the gay gene." There, she had said "it."

Her mother, lifting her glass up to her lips, paused, and then sipped. Her look reminded Leslie of a scene from the original *The Graduate*, when Mrs. Robinson tried to feign it all.

"Are they trying to cure it, or is this going to be just one more excuse for people to get away with their perversions?" Not taking her eyes off of Leslie, she took another sip, a longer sip, and set the glass down hard on the table; the wine sloshed.

"Guess I shouldn't have said anything." Leslie picked up her glass of wine, and for a fleeting moment she thought about getting stinking drunk, like she did the night her mother announced selling the company; and time before that, the day she buried Andrea. She knew what people meant when they said they were drowning in their sorrows, going so far off into all that you were feeling that it seemed easier to have some assistance in the emotional suicide than to find a way to swim back to yourself. At the moment, alcohol was the water she wanted to drown in.

The night of her mother's announcement about selling the company, she had left the party to go home, and while she was waiting for the light to change, she noticed a flashing sign, "Ladies' Night," at an old bar in Charlotte. Before the light changed, she made a quick right turn into the parking lot and got out of the car. As she walked to the front, two guys with long hair whistled at her.

"Damn," she heard one of them say.

"That woman's smokin', capital S," the other one said.

Leslie wondered whether they could tell she was angry or intended it as a compliment. She never found out, but she did find an empty bar stool and proceeded to get drunk on White Russians—one after another until she couldn't stop herself from slurring her words. She knew she was drunk after some guy walked up to her and introduced himself and asked her what her name was. "Leslie" came out "Lezzzzz,leee."

"Did you say you are a lezzie?"

She acted like she didn't hear him. When she swirled in the stool, and she could tell he wasn't standing there anymore, she wondered why he had said that.

She looked around the bar. Everyone seemed to enjoy the awful band that kept playing corny songs like "Tie a Yellow Ribbon 'Round the Old Oak Tree." At least everyone seemed to enjoy it except this guy sitting at the table closest to the band. Every time they finished a song. he'd yell, "ROCK-N-ROLL!"

"Jessssssss-ussssss," Leslie said to whoever might be listening. "I wisssssssh he would shut the hell up. He'sssss getting on my nervessss. Fact, maybe I'll jusssss walk over there and tell that redneck to ssssssshutup."

"He's not your type. Guess I wasn't either."

Leslie moved her bar stool to the right, the heels of her shoes locked onto the support of the stool. Tom, her boyfriend from college, was standing beside her, smiling. He always had a nice smile, she thought.

"Tom, remember?" he asked before she could translate her recognition into words. "God, you look great!"

"Tom, oh, sssssssweeet Thomassss. How you doing?" And she felt herself sliding off of the bar stool.

"Are you here with anyone?"

"Not iffff I can help it," she said as she tried to focus on his face.

"Let me drive you home."

"Thankssssss. That would probably be besssst."

She still couldn't recall portions of the drive to her place, just pieces, like a jigsaw puzzle she would fit together weeks later: embarrassing flashbacks. She remembered telling him about Andrea, sobbing uncontrollably, throwing up, calling her mother as many foul names as she could think of, and sleeping with him without worrying about who he had slept with since college or getting pregnant. It all just assisted in her drowning, she thought.

The next day, when she was throwing up every half hour and felt like someone had shot an expandable bullet through her head, she explained to Tom that she hadn't meant to use him. He had always been kind to her, but it just wasn't there for her. When he took her to her car and drove away, gentlemen that he had always been, she knew that part of her wild night was not only because of her mother's announcement, but because she had tried to prove to herself that she could be straight: Men didn't repulse her...they didn't, they never had. Even in her drunken stupor, Tom's touch had turned her on, the way he felt when he was on top of her; but, of course, that had only been in flashback moments.

Her secret life bothered her. It especially bothered her when she'd hear all of the gay jokes people made: the assumptions, so presumptuous, even more presumptuous than when some elderly white person in the grocery store would say a derogatory comment about a black person and assume that just because Leslie was white, she felt the same way. It was even worse with gay jokes. She had heard them all. She had become the queen of laughing the polite laugh and at the same time silently choking on losing another piece of her integrity. But on the rare occasions when she wanted to react—such as now at Morton's with her mother—she was always reminded, quickly, why she never should have said anything about "it" in the first place to her mother, and especially now, over dinner, when she didn't want the deal to close.

"I just had hoped you changed," her mother said.

"Changed?" Leslie set the wine glass down. She would be sober for this one.

"You haven't mentioned anyone in so long I was thinking that after your schoolgirl crush with..." She hesitated. "... you would find the right guy."

"Andrea. Her name was Andrea Harper, and we lived together for nine years, remember?"

"Shhhhhh. We *are* in a public place."

Leslie looked around the room. "I see that. My relationship with Andrea made your marriage with daddy, and every other sorry-ass date you've had since your divorce, a colossal joke!"

"Ladies?" The waiter stood beside the table. "Ready to order?"

Without asking Leslie what she wanted, her mother looked at the waiter and said, "We'll have two Caesar salads and the petite lobster dinner. Bring the salads with dinner."

"Very well."

They both watched the waiter walk away.

Her mother leaned forward, her breasts touching the edge of the white linen tablecloth. "You could change if you wanted."

"What should I do? Snap my fingers and say, 'Poof, all gone'?"

"You could see a therapist."

"I have seen a therapist."

"Perhaps you should ask for a refund, because obviously it didn't change you."

"Changing my sexuality was never part of the equation; surviving Andrea's death was."

"God works in mysterious ways."

"What does that mean?"

"Maybe God took Andrea away from you because 'it' is not right."

"Oh, so God has a personal vendetta against me?"

"I didn't say that."

"You might as well have."

"I'm simply trying to suggest that you could change. Maybe you should try this new cure that I've heard about. It's called the 'Exorsex Institute.'"

"'Exorsex Institute'? Let me guess," Leslie said. "It has

something to do with Jesus."

"I don't know all of the details, but it has helped hundreds of people just like you. Cured them. It took some work, but it is effective. Works better then the cure they had years ago."

"What cure, mother? I didn't realize you were such an expert on sexuality. I thought your expertise was just selling houses." Leslie decided to have another sip of wine.

"I once met someone they did it to."

"Did what to?"

Her mother took a sip of wine and scanned the room to make sure no one was listening. Still holding onto the stem of the glass, she leaned on the table, her thin brown eyebrows furrowed. Leslie thought her expression made her seem ten years older than she was.

"I'm going to tell you something," she said almost in a whisper, "something that I've never told anyone because I didn't understand it for a long time." She took another sip of wine, and as she swallowed, she breathed deeply. Leslie noticed how her nostrils flared. "In June 1941, when I was ten, your grandparents took me to New York City. We walked around Grand Central. I had never seen so many people in my life. People coming and going; all sorts of people. It was like a circus. I felt dizzy looking from one person to another, and then I noticed this young woman who had the creamiest skin I had ever seen, dressed in a beautiful pale blue dress, stockings, and black patent leather shoes, being escorted by two businessmen. They looked like they were lost. I watched them walk down one of the wings of the station."

Her mother took a sip of wine.

"I was sitting with mom and pop on a bench while they were studying a map trying to decide what sight we would go to next. I asked if I could go to the bathroom.

"I was in a stall and just pulling my panties back up and had flushed the toilet when I thought I heard someone close the door to the stall next to mine. Something slid toward my shoes. A wrinkled, white envelope made out to a Sumner Welles, State Department, Washington, D.C., with no return address, no stamp.

"She said, 'Help me. Please mail this for me.'

"I heard a knock on the door leading out into Grand Central, and then it creaked like someone partially opened it.

"'Everything okay, Rosemary?' some man asked.

"I heard her shoes click across the checkered tile floor. I peeked through a crack. It was that woman I had just seen."

Her mother took another sip of wine and stared hard at Leslie, like she was angry.

"Did you mail it?" Leslie asked.

"No."

"Open it?"

Her mother looked across the room for a moment.

"I kept it for a long time, tucked away in one of my diaries. I found it after you moved in with *her*. I opened it then. Rosemary, the girl who slid the letter across the floor, was pleading for this man to help her before her father sent her to some hospital in Washington for a lobotomy."

"What's the point mother?"

"The point *is*, who she was. She was the prettiest of them all."

"Of who?"

"The Kennedys. Rosemary Kennedy."

Leslie leaned forward. "Rosemary Kennedy? How do you know that?"

"One of the Kennedy girls got a lobotomy. This girl's name was Rosemary."

"Great," Leslie said. "I've got a mother who has surpassed any Kennedy conspiracy theory and thinks she met one of them on the way to a lobotomy. Wasn't she the one who was retarded?"

"Supposedly," her mother said, smugly.

"If she was so retarded, how could she..."

"Because maybe she wasn't. Maybe it was something else." Her mother looked around the room again. Leslie knew she was worried somebody might be listening. Appearances, like her phone voice, were still everything.

Her mother whispered between clenched teeth, "Do you know that back in the forties one of the cures for 'it' was a lobotomy?"

"'It'?"

"You know."

"Still can't say 'it,' can you, mother?"

Her mother rolled her eyes.

"What does this have to do with Rosemary Kennedy?"

"You figure it out."

"And you haven't you told anyone else about this?"

"No, because I don't want people to think I'm just one more crackpot making up stories about the Kennedy family."

"Why didn't you mail the letter?"

"I was a kid. It didn't have a stamp. It doesn't matter anyway. Things will never change, and neither will what people think. I don't want you to get fired one day over someone finding out about you."

"Maybe I won't get fired. Maybe they'll just sell the company right out from under me."

"That's not fair. It was a good offer."

"I *know* why you sold the company. Admit it."

"Okay, since you want the truth. I sold the company because I didn't want your lifestyle to damage everything I'd worked so hard for." Her mother twirled her empty wine glass by its stem.

"What did you think people were going to do? Yank their houses off the market?"

"It was a business decision."

"Maybe Rosemary's lobotomy was a business decision too." Leslie threw her napkin on the table and reached inside her purse. She tightly clutched the money, and then she laid two hundred-dollar bills next to her fork and got up from her seat.

"What's that for?"

"You figure it out."

THE WIZARD OF OZ

It was a night of leaving something, somewhere. Her mother at Morton's, and Squirrel still hunkered on top of the stool at The White House, probably still swigging beer and blowing out smoke between her missing incisors. Leslie locked the front door to the room, secured it with the bolt, and flung open the balcony door.

She lay in bed, on her back, like Andrea always did, looking at the ceiling.

She fell asleep in that position.

She dreamed about Andrea. A different dream than she usually had — ones in which she would see her as before, in life, and they would talk. Leslie would stop mid-sentence. "But you're dead."

"Thanks for reminding me," Andrea would say.

Leslie would always wake up after that part of the dream and have to turn a light on. She wasn't scared that Andrea would make a Patrick Swayze *Ghost* appearance, but death scared her. Forget all of the promises about eternal life; death was the bogeyman everyone should really be afraid of. Besides, if there was a God, and she hoped this was true, she was pissed. In a Ricky Ricardo voice, she said aloud, "God, you got a lot of 'splaining to do."

In this dream tonight, they were swimming around Diamond Head Rock, faster and faster, like the coyote chasing the roadrunner, until it wasn't clear who was chasing whom.

"See what happens if you don't keep up?" Andrea said before she flew out of the water and landed on top of the rocks. She was dressed like Glenda, the Good Witch, from *The Wizard of Oz.*

As Leslie hung onto the rocks, she saw her mother with a flying monkey on her shoulder. She was telling Andrea, "I'm going to get you, my little pretty."

Andrea tapped Leslie's mother on her shoulder with a wand, three times. Three midgets suddenly appeared and began singing, "Follow the Yellow Brick Road."

That was when she woke up.

She turned to look at the clock: 2:16 a.m.

She got out of bed and walked onto the balcony. It was high tide, and the moon beamed across the ocean and into the channel, casting its light across Valgooney's island.

Leslie heard a boat in the channel and squinted so she could see it better. The moon helped.

In the edges of the moonlight, she saw someone maneuver a small boat at Valgooney's dock, throw a cover over the engine, and sprint—and then dive into a pile of brush, just before another boat came zipping along the channel.

That boat slowed as it passed through the mouth of the channel and almost entered into the ocean. As the boat turned around, Leslie saw the words "Coast Guard" on its hull.

It sped back down the channel.

Even in the dark, Leslie could tell the crew was confused, but she wasn't. Valgooney Gore was the damn Crab Bandit, and at that moment, no one else knew it except for her.

THE ISLAND

After less than thirty minutes of watching the Coast Guard circle the channel past Valgooney's island, Leslie stole her mother's boat and a flashlight from her utility room. Okay, so it wasn't a perfect theft, because she would return the items. Maybe she'd tell her about it; maybe not. Or maybe her mother would see her boat docked at Valgooney's, because that's where it would be in another minute. Like her first impulse to put the real estate deal together two months ago, and to go to the gay bar tonight, Leslie followed this idea. From pajamas to shorts, T-shirt and tennis shoes, to running down the cement stairwell of the Hartford Motor Inn, down the deserted front street, to creeping beside her mother's house and onto the dock, she was going.

She had to admit that she hadn't ever felt quite like this before—that she was on a mission, and she had everything to lose. But for once, she didn't give a goddamn.

Besides, somebody had to tell Valgooney that she was going to get caught.

She didn't know the island would be as thick with trees and brush, but it was thicker than any forest Leslie had ever hiked in. She flicked on the flashlight to look for a way through the forest, past the dock.

A foot-thin, winding dirt path was to the left of the dock. It reminded her of the Appalachian Trail, only she could walk it in her light blue Nikes and not hiking boots. She followed it until she saw a light in the distance. At first it was dim, but the closer she came to it, the more clearly she saw it was two floodlights. One was shining on a huge, green sign hanging from a tree, like the kind you see on the highway for exits, only smaller, that read "No Bigots Allowed." Leslie laughed. Behind the sign, the trees and brush weren't as thick, and she saw the other light beaming through the trees toward her. She kept walking toward it, still following the thin trail.

She was surprised that she wasn't nervous, but after all that had happened that night, her anger was her fortress.

Valgooney sat in the window seat at the end of the trailer in the early morning darkness, and before she downed a shot of Cuervo Gold, she lifted her glass to herself: "To not getting caught." She leaned her head against the window and looked down onto the shadows of trees and brush. She liked being perched in this corner of the trailer, fourteen feet in the sky. It made her think about Tarzan and Jane. Maybe she should have a rope tied from trailer to tree, she thought, to swing down and yell.

She filled the shot glass with more tequila and was just raising it to toast to freeing more crabs, when there was a knock on the screen door. "Fuck," she thought to herself. It couldn't be the Coast Guard. Maybe she needed to be more careful about drinking Cuervo if somebody could walk up the wooden staircase without her hearing them.

She downed the tequila and slammed the shot glass on the kitchen table as she walked quickly through the living room. She was bracing herself for a nitwit in a uniform; and if she had to, she would charm him into submission.

Instead, as she approached the door, the lamp cast a yellow glow onto Leslie's face.

Valgooney frowned and cocked her head to the side.

"Ms. Gore. Just thought you'd like to know you missed the Coast Guard by one minute." As Leslie turned to leave, and the top stair creaked.

"How do you know my name?" Valgooney crossed her arms.

Leslie turned back around. "Earl. Tim Lewis, from the *Sun Times*. You're going to get arrested."

"For riding the channels at night?" Valgooney still stood behind the screen door, arms still crossed, as she tried to suppress a smile.

"I think it's called 'destruction of private property.' I'm surprised that no one else has figured out that you're the Crab Bandit. That's all I wanted to tell you. Good night, or maybe I should say, 'good morning.'"

Leslie turned completely around, and when her tennis shoes landed on the next step, she heard the screen door creak. Valgooney walked onto the front stoop, arms uncrossed.

"You're not going to turn me in for the $25,000 reward." She didn't say it like a question.

Leslie, still descending the stairs, stopped. "No, I've always admired the rebel in others." Leslie turned to face her.

Valgooney smiled. "Who are you?"

"Just a nobody commercial real estate broker."

"Oh, one of those people. You're probably interested in…."

But Leslie cut her short. "No, I don't want to broker your land. At the moment, I don't want to broker another deal for the rest of my life."

"In that case, and since you don't even want the reward money, would you care for some coffee? Tequila?"

Valgooney was smiling, but it wasn't just her lips that smiled. Even in the partial darkness, with the floodlight shining on the ground below and the light inside the doorway, she knew what Tim meant about her eyes. Andrea had the striking long eyelashes, but Valgooney had sea eyes. Tim hadn't told Leslie that you could probably hear the ocean in those eyes.

"Whatever you're drinking," she said.

Leslie also knew what Tim meant when he said Valgooney was incredibly fit and how it almost killed him. Though she imagined she was in much better shape than Tim, after they left the trailer with a bottle of Tequila and two shot glasses, they hiked to the ocean side of her island. The trail dead-ended into a row of sand dunes at least twenty feet high, all covered with thick brownish grass. Leslie thought they looked like ice cream cones dipped in chocolate. She walked up a dune and was out of breath when she reached the top. Not Valgooney. She didn't even appear to need to breathe.

They sat on top of the dune, in silence, after that first shot of Cuervo. Leslie thought it was ironic that they were drinking tequila, and Cuervo at that. The universe was toying with her, it had to be, she thought, because she was feeling as insecure as she had the night she told Andrea how she felt about her. Whatever brave momentum had struck her at dinner with her mother earlier tonight, stopped for refueling when she met Squirrel, and escalated after stealing the boat and racing across the channel—all that brought her to this moment—suddenly left without saying 'good-bye.' Not even Cuervo could help her.

"Care for another?" Valgooney asked.

"Sure. What's a hangover, anyway?"

"Once in a while, I think it's okay to get on the left side of some Tequila."

She filled Leslie's glass and then hers. They let their glasses click, and then they both drank the shot.

"Thanks for not turning me in to the Coast Guard."

"I love that you've got them stumped." As Leslie said this, she remembered how she and Andrea used to laugh at some of the men who would come onto them, oblivious to the subtle clues of their life together. But why would they, or should they, she wondered now. It was a stupid game. She and Andrea should have been honest and quit subjecting the unassuming men to an ego decapitation.

Once, though, Andrea decided to be honest with another teacher who wouldn't take "no" for an answer, even when she repeatedly told him she wasn't interested in him. "Why?" Delmar would ask. "I know you don't have a boyfriend." So she decided to tell him the truth. Instead of respecting her for telling him, he told the principal and tried to get her fired. He didn't stop there. He made sure that all of the teachers in the school knew about her personal life. He started spreading rumors that she liked little girls.

"If you're going to keep spreading rumors, at least get your nouns right. I am not a pedophile; I'm a lesbian."

She told Leslie that he didn't respond, but he practically sprinted down the hallway, like a roach running into the nearest escape after someone turned on the light.

At least Andrea was professional about the entire episode. She set up an appointment with the principal and told him that as long as she did her job and did it well, her personal life was her own business. The principal agreed but told her that it would be a while before things would blow over.

Some of the teachers remained as friendly as they had always been, but there were a few who whispered behind her back, as if she couldn't hear them, as if lesbianism had made her deaf. Then there were those who acted as if Andrea had a contagious disease. She heard that a teacher started spraying the faculty phone with a disinfectant after Andrea used it.

Andrea didn't know which was worse: the covert or the overt.

After another teacher announced his engagement, Andrea walked up to him and said, "How about a congratulatory hug?" He looked at her like he was surprised and said, "You don't mind hugging men?"

When she ran into Delmar again in the hallway, she said, "Even if I were interested in you, you have a severe character flaw."

He glared at her and said, "No, babe. You're the one who's messed up. And the best part? You're going straight to hell for it."

She moved close to his face and said, "You're as worthless as the foreskin on your dick."

As Leslie sat on top of the dunes with Valgooney, with the hint of the morning sun barely peeping above the horizon, she felt angry that she still lived her life this way: still dealing with an anger, like lava, seeping and wanting to erupt into action. For once in her stale, safe life, she wanted something, anything, to change. She poured another shot of tequila, leaned her head back and swallowed.

Leslie looked again at the faint pink sky. *I'm going to tell her*, she thought. *Wash away the need to stump. Wash this deal out. No, damn sink it.*

"Would you like another cause, Ms. Gore? De-Nazi-ize some people? I'll tell you about the sellout of the century and what an asshole I really am if I don't stop it."

Valgooney reached for the bottle that was stuck in the sand and then filled their glasses.

Leslie picked a clump of sand and let it fall through her fingers as she finished saying, "...so maybe my mother couldn't have realized the import of her letter, but when she did, it was too late, and shall I add, she didn't really give a damn until my life haunted her for hoarding that letter. All I know is, I can't stand by waiting for the world to finish off me and their Rosemary's. It makes me want to scream."

"Go for it," Valgooney said.

Leslie wondered if a scream could ride a wave across the channel and into her mother's bedroom where she probably was still sleeping; and if the scream stopped there, would her mother wake up and see what a scream looked like: full of fear, with a comet's tail? But her fear didn't visit every seventy-five years. Hers was a permanent constellation.

After Valgooney walked Leslie to her boat, she went back to the dunes and lay on her back, drunk and sleepy. God, she thought, she had missed an entire night of sleep. Sometimes when she couldn't sleep, she would leave the trailer in the middle of the night and fall asleep on top of the dunes, sometimes waking to a sky that looked as if a painter had hurled pink and burgundy paint onto a baby blue backdrop.

As Valgooney lay on her back, she smiled, thinking that the evening turned out in a way that she couldn't have predicted. She really had thought she was going to get arrested when she heard that knock on her door; but instead, her first female friendship in years began on the steps to her trailer and on the top of her dune.

It's not that she shunned friendships with women; it's just that she found most women superficial. Leslie was different. Leslie was about more than herself.

Valgooney sat up and watched another row of clouds float by, and then the waves fold over as they rolled onto the shore. She understood their fervor; fervor with a purpose in mind. She knew you couldn't change the fervor. Your only choices were to ignore it and fall victim to its wet pounce, or ride its rhythm. That's why she was going to help Leslie with her complicated real estate deal.

Something had to wash Rosemary Kennedy ashore.

BEHIND THE SCENES

"**R**everend Snead? Ron Reilly, from Schorr Laboratories, is here to see you."

Ralph Snead pushed the button on his phone, the one sitting on top of his brand-new desk—the one he made his organization pay for...the organization that made him wealthy because he knew how to woo the Republicans and how to silence the liberals. Didn't almost all the candidates that he chose get into office during the last four elections? So he didn't feel guilty about the desk or some of his other perks.

"Send him in."

Ralph stood up behind his desk as the secretary opened the door.

"Ron, to what do I owe the honor of this visit?" Ralph walked around the desk and toward Ron.

The secretary closed the door as Ron shook Ralph's hand. "I'm not making a donation this time."

"God said that it's more blessed to give than to receive."

"Know what I think, Reverend? I think whoever wrote that was dyslexic."

Ralph laughed. He pointed to a chair as he walked back around his desk and sat back down.

"Thought everything was fine after your company caused such a stir with that gay gene discovery." He snorted. "Gay gene, right. The only gay gene I've ever seen was a gay man in jeans." Ralph laughed at his own play on words.

"This is a courtesy call. We've found the ultimate cure, if you can call it that." Ron leaned back in the chair and ran his right hand down his mustache. "The best thing about science is that it doesn't discriminate; it just is. But the Christians? The sins they pick to exploit are the hemorrhoids of life. I find it rather amusing."

Ralph leaned back in his chair and crossed his arms. "I'm already fixing them. Got a whole operation that 'exorsexes' the gay demon." He leaned back in his chair. "In fact, let me educate you about power—the power of God." Ralph turned around and pushed an electrical switch on the wall behind him. "Look over here," he said as he pointed to a wall where a wide screen rolled down. "Watch this."

A video began playing, a video with Ralph's voice; a voice that Ron thought sounded like an extra-nasal Al Frankin.

"Are you gay? Are you the father, mother, sibling, or friend of a homosexual?" (When he said "homosexual," he enunciated every syllable, so it sounded like "ho-mo-sex-u-al"). "Are you using your homosexuality as a way to keep you from the Kingdom of God and Jesus?" His "Jesus" sounded like "Gee-zus."

"If you answered 'yes' to any of these questions, then the 'Exorsex Institute' may be the place you're looking for. Homosexuality is a sin, a disease, and a cancer on the soul. Only through the power of God can you be healed of this sickness. Meet John and Amy, who know the power of God."

The caption "John" flashed on the screen. John, a young man in his thirties, sat next to an elderly woman.

John spoke: "I used to do all sorts of terrible things. Used to go to gay bars, gay movies. I couldn't escape the lifestyle until I came to the Institute."

The elderly woman looked right into the camera.

"I knew from an early age that my son wasn't normal. He played with dolls, cried a lot, and worst of all, he listened to Bette Midler. I tried to do something: karate lessons, sports camps. Fixed him up with dozens of girls from our church."

John and his mother looked at each other and laughed, a staged laugh that Ron thought sounded like canned laughter from a sitcom. "My mother didn't know that these things wouldn't change me, until I found this Institute."

The video shows Ralph in a three-piece suit. He narrates again.

"Now meet Amy." (Even "Amy" was enunciated).

The video flashed to a striking young woman, dressed like she was going to a prom.

"I was a tomboy. I loved power tools, sports. I loved women. I panted for k.d. lang. I couldn't imagine being with a man until I came to the Institute."

The camera stayed focused on her as Ralph narrated again.

"Watch the power of God at work."

The camera flashed back to John, but this time, the caption read, "John six months earlier." John was dressed in a pink button-down shirt, and cutoff shorts so short and tight that you could see the outline of his penis. His voice was higher-pitched and more nasal than in the first part of the video, and he flipped his hands around as he said, "I hope Jesus can help me." ("I," flip of the hand, "hope," flip of the hand, "Jesus," flip of the hand, "can," flip of the hand, "help," flip of the hand, "me," hand rests.)

As the camera merged the "old John" with the "new John," Ralph narrated again.

"Patients at our institute undergo an intensive six-week treatment program. We study God's word." As he continued to narrate, the camera flashed to a teacher lecturing with a Bible in his right hand. Two men quickly exchanged glances. The teacher said, "Men don't exchange glances. Men always look straight ahead."

The camera moved to another scene: inside a large sanctuary. Men and women had their arms raised, shouting, "Take it, Jesus." A woman fell into the aisle, shaking and shouting, "Jesus has taken it! Jesus has taken it!"

Ralph said, "Once they've been delivered, we teach men and women their proper God-given roles."

The camera moved to a room where a group of women were all wearing dresses and high heels; some were obviously uncomfortable. They squirmed. Others were sitting down, but not properly—their legs were spread too far and wide apart. The teacher slapped their legs with a black Bible.

The teacher said, "Repeat after me: 'Smile.'"

She waited while the class said "smile" in unison.

"'Be pleasant.'"

"'Be pleasant.'"

"'Laugh at all his jokes.'"

"'Laugh at all his jokes.'"

"And most importantly, class, 'Let him win.'"

"'Let him win.'"

"Remember, it's all for Jesus!" The teacher smiled long and wide.

Ralph leaned further back in his chair and pushed a button. The video stopped.

Ron said, "I hate to be the one to end your money-making business, but once we start correcting this genetic fuck-up before birth, you're going to run out of homosexuals." (Ron said "homosexuals" like Ralph had in the video).

Ralph leaned across his desk, carefully moving his wrist so that his watch didn't scratch the surface. "No. I hate to be the one to tell you that the entire Christian community from coast to coast is gonna do whatever I say." He pointed his finger at his chest when he finished the sentence.

Ron pulled at his mustache. "Meaning?"

"You call it science. We call it God. You call it genetics. We call it sin. You think you save the world with science, but we save it with religion."

"I don't give a damn about your 'religion.'"

"People don't want science. People want God," Ralph said.

Ron stood halfway up in his chair. "For Christ's sake! We all want the same thing—power!"

Ralph pointed his finger at Ron. "You start messing around with God's playing field, and we'll tie up your project until you're too old to breed."

Ron stood up, and as he did, the chair moved. "Let me tell you something, Reverend. The reason I came here today was to get your 'okay.' Not that I needed it. But if you don't support what we're getting ready to do, I'll take all of the business away from you. See, we are going to have mandatory clinics for expecting mothers, and once we get the APA's ruling, it's done." Ron moved closer to the desk. "It's like this: We'll put a stop to it at birth—you'll still get the homo that was born yesterday. Plenty for all."

XENOPHOBIC: A BIG WORD THAT I USED TO SPELL

Maybe, maybe, I wasn't the best speller, but neither were my brothers. Some families share the same missing tooth, tooth; other families share secrets, secrets. Mine used to share big, wide smiles, bad spelling, and secrets that weren't really secrets. Sometimes, when they wheel me in to watch the news, my family is in the news, news. Sometimes, when my family, family is in the news, the staff doesn't think that I can make the connections. I just can't tell you what I know, know, but because of what they did to me. How can something, something be a secret when it's on the news? Everybody knew that I wasn't, wasn't retarded. You don't, don't send your oldest daughter to look after a younger sister, if, if they are retarded, do you? You don't get to meet, meet with royalty or the president, do you, if you're retarded? Take a look at our family pictures, sometime. You decide, decide if I was a debutante or retarded. Then I'll tell you some secrets that aren't secrets. But, I'll start with this: when I wrote *her* my good-bye letter. I told her that Father had given up on a psychiatrist. Can a doctor cut out love, love?

"IT AIN'T CHEESE"

Valgooney told Earl she had some business to take care of and that he wouldn't be able to reach her for a week. She took the Amtrak from Myrtle Beach to Madison, Wisconsin, and from there, she got a rental car and drove to Watts Living Care Center in Bonduel.

Valgooney could hear Lola now. She would say to Earl, "Wisconsin? Lord, what the girl up to now?"

"It ain't cheese," she envisioned him saying.

Valgooney also knew that when Lola found out later that she had taken the train, she would tease her about her fear of flying. Flying was never an option for her.

They had argued this too many times, at night, sitting on their front porch.

"More people die in car accidents," Lola said, crossing her arms without having to say Valgooney was stupid for saying she would never fly. "Beside, when it your time to go, the Man gonna come and get you, no matter what." Then Lola mumbled something under her breath and said, "I jest don't get how someone as smart as you don't make no sense sometimes."

Valgooney thought about this conversation as she drove the rental car to Bonduel.

She was only following her premonition. But she never tried to explain that to Lola. Lola was too conventional about her Christianity to understand that there might be a difference between destiny and free will, and maybe these things unwittingly clashed every once in a while. Besides, God would be awfully busy to oversee every tiny thing.

When she arrived in Bonduel, it felt hard to breathe between the buildings, asphalt, and people. There was no repetitious sound like the ocean to lull people into a different place, into the quiet of themselves, if they would ever listen.

Posing as a daughter seeking a place for her mother whose Alzheimer's was in the last stage, she was given the grand tour by Kendall Wentz, the public relations facilitator.

While she waited for him, she looked at the plaques on the wall. Several were in honor of the Kennedy family. The Kennedy plaques were encased in a mahogany frame.

"Ms. Gore?" He walked toward where she was standing, reading the plaques.

She nodded, still looking at the plaques. Then she turned around to shake his hand. "Thanks for meeting with me. I know you must be a busy man." She felt him shake as he shook her hand.

Good, she thought. An easy sexual conquest, if needed.

He looked like Barney Fife; she hoped he was like Barney Fife. All she would have to do is smile a little, maybe occasionally stand a little closer to him, and she knew he would be butter. That was the only thing she didn't like about men. They weren't a challenge. Whatever you wanted was yours. The biggest of the egos could get drunk on an ounce of flattery and a teaspoon of flirt.

"So, you would like to have your mother be considered for our facility?"

Julie E. Townsend

"Yes, if at all possible."

"There's a waiting list." He puffed his chest out a little.

Definitely Barney Fife, she thought to herself. "I'm sure there is. The place seems exquisite from the buildings to the grounds. It must take a lot of your time to make sure all of this is run properly and smoothly." She inched a little closer to him.

"It's just one of the many things we pride ourselves on." When he said this, he jutted his jaw out like Barney, as if he personally attended the grounds. Andy Griffith didn't run that jail; he did.

She nodded toward one of the larger wooden plaques. "Are the Kennedy's contributors?"

"You might say they have a vested interest."

She moved even closer to him, but he didn't back away. "Really?"

He leaned near her, lowered his voice and said, "Rosemary Kennedy is a permanent resident."

"So if my mother lives here, she'll be rubbing walking canes with the famous?"

Still standing close, he continued. "Mostly she keeps to herself. But an attendant wheels her out on the grounds every morning, rain or shine. Care to take a tour?"

"Are you sure you have the time?"

"I'll make time," he said. He smoothed back his hair with both hands.

Kendall jutted out his elbow, and Valgooney wrapped her hand around it. She could feel his arm vibrate. Kendall began pointing to the plants and sculptured bushes, while Valgooney politely nodded as she wondered how long it had been since she had slept with any of the tourists. The urge was still there, but since Joe had left town, and after that night with Leslie on the dunes, her shallow seductive urges were moving into something she couldn't quite define. Maybe it was time to give something up for Lent, even though she had missed that by many months. She wouldn't seduce this Kendall wimp. He wasn't worth the information that she could find through other means, flirting or not.

After she and Kendall walked for a while longer, he suggested getting into one of the brand-new golf carts. She agreed, but insisted that he was taking entirely too much of his precious time with her and what a sweetheart of a man he was.

He had only smiled and put one of his arms around the back of the short seat, slightly touching the edge of her shoulder.

Valgooney thought that her island could look like this manicured place if she ever cleared off the brush and trees. But she liked nature's kind of lush, without any help from lawn mowers and weed eaters.

When Kendall brought the cart to a stop to make sure she saw the new fountain, she saw an attendant wheeling a woman in a wheelchair on the sidewalk, coming toward them.

"...And next year, we're going to install another one over there." Kendall pointed near where the attendant was pushing the woman in the chair. He leaned close to Valgooney.

"That's Rosemary, since you were interested."

The attendant wheeled past them, but instead of staring at Rosemary, Valgooney focused on the attendant's name tag: "Stek."

"She's been here a long time," Kendall was saying. For a second, Valgooney thought he sounded like he felt sorry for her, but then he began launching into the other projects the facility planned to do, still maintaining his ego-laden façade. But that was okay with her, because she now had a contact name. She wondered if Mr. Stek needed some extra cash. A lot of extra cash.

Julie E. Townsend

"Let me get this straight," William Wiley said. "You, who gave me a lecture about Pat Robertson, want to kidnap *the* Rosemary Kennedy?"

"I know. But this is for a different reason, one that you'll want to be part of," Valgooney said as she sipped on coffee at Fullwood's Diner, where they had first met a couple of years ago.

"Refresh my memory. Isn't that the Kennedy who is retarded? Why her?"

"I can't you tell you exactly why right now. It's going to be made public the day of the march."

"Tell me more about this march. You're going to need my networking skills for this one."

"That's why we're here." She smiled at him. "We're going to amass the largest march that's ever been held for gay rights, but I've seen the news footage of other gay rights marches, and all the media ever shows are the freaks with their tongues down each other's throats. I say we manipulate the media for a change. See, I envision a march on a Dr. Martin Luther King, Jr., level. They marched in their Sunday clothes, held their heads high. Those who marched with him were nothing like the images playing in the minds of most Americans, so it made the racists look like mean-ass idiots."

"Are you gay?" Wiley stared hard at her.

"No," she said quickly before she took a sip of a coffee so that he wouldn't see her to break into a smile. *Are you gay?* She ran the words back through her head. Did it mean she was gay when, the entire way back from Wisconsin, all she could think about was what Leslie would think of her plan; that is, if she told her? Did it mean she was gay because all she wanted to do was sit on the dunes with her and listen to her talk more about her life and how she loved Andrea? Did it mean she was gay just because she wanted to get to know a gay woman? Did it mean she was gay because she thought Leslie was cute and charming? If it did, then there sure were a hell of a lot of gay people in the world. The whole damn world was gay.

Wiley took another sip of his coffee, setting the cup down a little too hard, she thought. "How am I supposed to tell a bunch of queens they can't dress in drag for this thing? I'll risk getting run over by the 'dykes on bikes.'"

"Every once in a while, convention has its place. Tell them that."

"What's so important about it?"

Valgooney leaned in close to him and whispered, "Because in less than a month, a research company is going to buy the former base in Myrtle, and they're going to do some experiments on homosexuals."

"You're kidding."

"Was Hitler kidding?" She still leaned in close.

William shook his head. "We're evil, you know. We work, pay taxes, try to keep our love indoors, sequestered from co-workers, would-be friends and family members who blame us for all of the world's dysfunction. Yeah. We're evil."

Valgooney could feel his anger across the table. It reminded her of Leslie's, and of David Farnsworth's fight with his father—of always having to defend oneself against some never-ending enemy.

"So, will you help me with the march on Myrtle?"

"March on Myrtle," he said. "It sounds festive." He smiled and repeated it. "March on Myrtle. I like the sound of it."

The Cherry Grove pier rocked in the night breeze. Leslie sat on one of the high wooden benches, built for fishermen's backs, not hers, so she squirmed, trying to get into a different position that didn't hurt her back or butt.

Valgooney had been quiet about what she was planning. Leslie appreciated her efforts, but she wished that Valgooney would tell her more. It made Leslie feel like she did sometimes when she worked with other brokers on a deal—like she was only in the deal in some small capacity, when really she was out of the loop.

The worst part for her was having to keep up the façade of doing the deal and enduring another dinner with Ron Reilly, who had insisted on taking her to dinner earlier that night. His staff had flown in for the final inspections of the base.

She had to watch his mustache bob up and down as he chewed on his prime rib. She thought he ate it like a hungry dog. He certainly slurped his wine like he was licking it out of a doggie bowl. Then, as he shoved another piece of steak into his mouth, part of its blood ran down the edges of his mustache and hung there, like it couldn't decide whether to jump ship or not. She was just waiting for it to fling onto her side of the table. *Yuck*, she had thought. Why didn't he finger that juice away?

Instead, the juice hung as he kept going on and on about the real estate deal.

She hated the way he made her feel—more of a hypocrite than she already was. When would she cease caring if people found out she was a lesbian? Did her little life really alter anyone else's? Just when did gays become the international boogeymen, boogeywomen, boogeyfags, boogeydykes, boogey-damn-gays?

What she really wanted to do was say, "Hey, Reilly, guess what? I'm a boogey-fem-lesbian. Boo!" But she couldn't, because if she did, all of the anger that led her to this point might sabotage the sabotage.

After the dinner, she had headed to the pier, where she now sat. She grabbed onto the pier's plank and let her fingernails dig deep and hard into the wood.

Why, Leslie thought, would someone as young, beautiful, smart, and rich as Valgooney need such a shallow fill? What was it about her mother and Valgooney that made them make such poor choices?

MARCH ON MYRTLE

Jim Swain, a news reporter, adjusted his microphone.

"At the cue, ready?" a cameraman said.

He nodded.

"They're calling this the largest march *ever* for gay rights. The crowd is projected at three million. Every hotel room and campground within a seventy-five-mile radius is booked. Bob? Susan? Back to you."

Inside the studio, Bob and Susan were sitting behind the anchor desk. They looked at Jim on a small screen.

"Where are they marching to?" Bob asked.

The camera flashed back to Jim. Holding his hand closer to his ear, Jim said, "The old military base. We learned just a few minutes ago that the base is under contract with a research facility in Houston. What we don't know yet is whether there is a connection, and why the marchers are holding the rally at the entrance to the base. Bob? Susan?"

Susan said, "We understand that Oprah, Barbara Streisand, k.d. lang and Melissa Etheridge are at the rally. Any confirmation on that?"

"We've heard the same thing. No sightings yet. Want me to get their autographs?"

The camera flashed back to Bob and Susan in the studio. They laughed.

"Bob, Susan, let's switch to Jim at the scene. Apparently, there's some commotion at the entrance of the base."

Elvin, a spectator, stood in front of the gates to the base. Behind him, the Reverend Farnsworth—whose gut, packed into a red T-shirt, extended at least nine inches over his belt, as if he were with child—was holding a fire hose. His shirt read, "Jesus is Love." Thirty other people helped him hold the hose.

"Elvin, could you tell us what just happened?" Jim asked.

"That preacher guy right there made somebody real mad. Somebody needs to call the police." Elvin said it like "po-leese."

"Thank you," Jim said, and then to the camera, "Bob, the Reverend Farnsworth, whose show, 'Jesus-4-U,' is here protesting the march. He just got into an argument with one of the marchers. Back to you." The camera stopped for a second on Farnsworth's red baseball cap that also read, "Jesus is Love."

L ola had some spittle hovering in the corner of her mouth. "Humph. Nerve of that man."

She was walking with Earl and some people in the march, when Farnsworth kept shouting, "You're all going to hell."

Lola shouted back, "The only hell they is—is the hate in you."

Farnsworth, sweat rolling down his face, walked closer to Lola. "Not according to God Almighty! Everyone of you is going to burn in the eternal flame of Satan's sin!"

She stuck her finger near his nose just like she had done to Simmons years ago. "If they a sin here, it the way you treatin' people. God's love never give you the license to hate. You done twisted it to hell and back again!"

She knew Earl was standing behind her.

"Honey, anything you wanna add?"

"Think you 'bout say it all."

Then she moved closer to Farnsworth, so close that she could smell his sweat beating through his red T-shirt. He smelled like onions. "Why, you ain't nothin' but a Bible-totin' Grand Master of the KKK," she said.

"They said it couldn't be done, that no one cares about you. But look around you," the spokeswoman said into the microphone on the stage looking out over thousands of people.

The crowd clapped.

"Before Melissa sings, we've asked William Wiley of the World Gay Alliance to say a few words." The spokeswoman looked to the side of the stage.

The crowd began clapping.

Wiley walked across the stage and up to the microphone stand. The crowd looked like a sea of people: heads moving at the same exact time.

"They claim that homosexuals want to convert others to their lifestyle. Is there some queer Billy Graham crusade where you plead for others to join your lifestyle so that they, too, can be discriminated against? Are there Uncle Sam posters pointing a limp-wristed finger saying, 'We Want You?'"

The audience laughed. Valgooney, who was standing at the base of the stage stairs, was surprised at how loud millions of laughs sounded. It was as if they were all laughing into the microphone.

"Well, is there?" Wiley asked.

The crowd collectively yelled, "No!"

"Let me tell you what kind of group is out there, sanctioned by our government, the religious Nazis, and the latest claims about homosexuality. Schoor, a research company that has this base under contract, plans to alter who you are, and each knows what the other is doing. Don't think for one minute that the government didn't know what Schoor and Ralph Sneed's ministry want to do."

A murmur began in the crowd, and Valgooney could see the sea of faces turning side-to-side, like they weren't quite sure if they heard him correctly, so they were confirming it with the people beside them. As she turned to look back at Wiley, she saw Leslie trying to inch toward her. She waved and turned to listen.

He continued. "They're making sure that homosexuality is put back on the list as a mental illness. That gives them clearance for their next procedure."

The crowd's murmurs sounded like thunder, a low thunder, the first-warning-of-a-storm kind of thunder.

"As far as their next procedure, you wouldn't believe me if I told you, but you will be able to read the entire story in tomorrow's *Sun Times*. Tim Lewis is doing the story." He paused. "But here's what I hope you'll join me for at one o'clock today: We're going to march down to the federal courthouse, and you're each going to...." But before he finished making his point, he grabbed the microphone stand, pulled it closer to him, and shouted, "SUE!"

The audience began chanting, "SUE, SUE, SUE."

Wiley let go of the stand and walked toward the side stage. The crowd stood on their feet and began clapping, still chanting, "SUE, SUE, SUE."

When he walked down the stairs, the musical score for "People Who Need People" began playing. Leslie stood next to Valgooney, but she got pushed aside by the news reporters who rushed toward Wiley.

They all seemed to say his name in unison; their questions merged into one, like a six-lane highway quickly shrinking into two.

"Mr. Wiley, do you know for a fact what the plans are for the base?"

As he began answering that question, through the faces and microphone, Leslie saw Valgooney smiling at her. Valgooney nodded toward the ocean.

Wiley said loudly to the reporters, "If you want to know anything else, see Tim Lewis over there with *The Sun Times*. He has the exclusive."

The reporters turned to look where he was pointing. Tim was leaning against a post, watching them. He smiled.

They sprinted toward him, cameras and all.

Leslie thought the reporters looked like a flock of seagulls following a shrimp boat, hoping for a bite of the goods.

"Come on," Valgooney said.

The crowd roared as a drag queen who looked like Barbra Streisand began singing "People Who Need People."

Leslie glanced back up toward the stage, and she thought he/she looked so real, that maybe it was Barbra.

Valgooney turned to look at Leslie as they meandered through the crowd, and she said, "That song gets on my nerves."

"I know what you mean."

PAST THE CROWD

By the time Valgooney and Leslie made it onto the beach, Barbra Streisand—or the look-alike—had finished singing. Leslie didn't want to make the same sexual mistake she had so many years ago with the John Travolta look-alike woman. The crowd roared again in the distance.

Valgooney turned to Leslie. "What happened at the closing table?"

"It was beautiful," she said. "Just after Major Johnson signed some documents, Reilly was drooling. I've never seen someone drool."

"I said, 'Reilly, as your agent, I'm going to advise you not to sign.'"

"What, the hell?" Johnson shouted.

"I said, 'The deal will backfire on you.'"

"Reilly wiped the corners of his mouth. 'Backfire?'" Leslie looked over at Valgooney, who had stopped walking and who was listening intently, furrowed brows and all.

"I turned to the closing attorney and asked if he had a TV there or a radio. Of course, they're all looking at me like I'm crazy. Reilly looked pissed by then, rubbed his mustache, and yanked my arm. 'What's going on here?'"

"The news. We've got to watch the news," I told him.

"He let go of my arm. We all walked down to the next room and saw the first reports of the marchers heading to the base. It was beautiful. The news chopper showed the entire span of marchers. The major told Reilly that the government would sue them if he didn't sign the papers. And Reilly told Johnson to go fuck himself." Leslie laughed. "Then the major told me that he'd make sure I'd lose my license in every state I was licensed in."

"Can he do that?" Valgooney asked.

Leslie shrugged. "Maybe, but his grounds aren't strong. I'd claim that I was only fulfilling my duties as a buyer's agent. But I did get to say something I've always wanted to say to men in business." Leslie smiled as she retold the scene from that morning. "I told Major Johnson that he was constipated, and as Reilly laughed at that, I turned to him and said that I hoped his firstborn was the biggest fucking fag that ever pranced the face of the earth!"

Valgooney laughed. "You didn't."

"Oh, there's more. As I closed up my briefcase, I told Reilly that I had leaked what his company was going to do, and that everyone would consider it forced abortion. He grabbed my arm and called me a 'fag-lesbian-lover.'"

The water lapped up near them when they noticed three men wearing dark blue business suits and talking into hand-held radios walking toward them. When one of them, a short, fat man with brown hair, got closer, he looked hard at Valgooney, as if she were some criminal and, if needed, he could blow her away on a second's notice.

"Ms. Gore?"

"Last time I checked," she said.

"You're under arrest for the attempted kidnapping of Rosemary Kennedy." He opened his wallet: FBI.

"What the hell?" Leslie said.

Valgooney looked at her. Her face was expressionless, but Leslie knew it meant to shut up. Andrea had perfected those looks.

The other men handcuffed Valgooney as the fat man held onto the edge of her elbow and pushed her toward a dark blue Crown Victoria, parked in a beach access alley. Leslie walked with her, trying to stay by her side, but one of the men made sure she didn't get too close. What was she going to do? she thought.

When they got to the car, they pushed Valgooney's head down hard, so she could go into the back seat. She turned to Leslie and yelled, "Find Earl. He'll know who to reach."

A DIFFERENT STROLL

Today when that young man took me for my stroll around the grounds, he seemed kind of nervous, nervous. It wasn't so much that he shook, shook, when he lifted me into the wheelchair, it was all in his eyes, eyes, like he was contemplating something—something that he wasn't convinced about—was he wondering, wondering, whether it was a good thing. It reminded me of the look one of father's men had when we boarded the train at Grand Central. If father would have seen his look, look, he may have pulled him off the job. Father didn't have the look. Because Father always had the same look: a fixed season, season, if there is such a thing.

The attendant wheeled me faster, faster, than he normally does. And then a strange thing happened. He took a different route than he usually does, and he didn't say a word. That was another sign, sign. Normally, he talks the whole way. I talk to him, too, although he never seems to hear me, me. Once he said to me, "Ms. Rosemary, do you ever get mad? I mean the kind of mad that you know you could choke someone just because they opened their mouths? The kind of mad that knows no cure?"

I told him we weren't allowed to be mad, mad, but that because I had, had, I was here. Silenced. He acted like he didn't hear me. Although I know I'm speaking. I can hear every word, every word, in my mind.

He took another sidewalk, pushing me along, along, but not saying anything until we saw a car pull up near one of the side entrances. He said, "I don't know why I'm doing this. But she said this was just the exclamation mark that she needed. She promised me that you'd be fine. And this woman that will be picking you up, well Ms. Rosemary, she's supposed to treat you like a queen."

I asked, "Where are we going, going?"

He didn't hear me, me.

Kendall was screaming, screaming, "Police, somebody call the police!"

JAIL BAIT

As Leslie opened the door to her hotel room, the phone was ringing.

"Hello?" Leslie said.

"Heard you were on the national news. You do know that you're probably going to lose your real estate license? Just *had* to embarrass me, didn't you?"

They hadn't spoken since Morton's, two months ago.

"It's not about you, mother. Not everything that happens in this world is about you."

"God, I am *so* embarrassed."

"Really? Well, your bigotry embarrasses me." Leslie slammed the phone down.

They didn't know when Valgooney could post bond; the female officer with her hair in a tight bun had told Leslie, "Might be two hours, might be tomorrow."

She walked down the street looking for something to eat. Everything was closed. It was just like Charlotte, she thought, 6:35 p.m. and most of the life-force moved out to the suburbs, no matter what they claimed about an "alive uptown, downtown, or midtown." When it came down to it, Charlotte was still a southern city. Southerners liked their daily respites, lawns, commutes and all. Myrtle Beach was no different, especially when the summer season was over; however, she was surprised that the marchers hadn't found their way to this part of the Grand Strand.

She walked backed to the county jail, trying not to think too much about Valgooney's arrest. She figured out why Valgooney tried to do it—if she had gotten away with wheeling Rosemary on stage in front of millions, the march would have had an even greater impact. What an "outing" that would have been!

As Leslie entered the jail, a female officer standing behind a glassed-in window barely glanced up at her.

Earl and a woman were sitting on one of the benches near the window.

Earl stood up when he saw Leslie.

He turned to Lola. "Honey, this here is Leslie."

Lola nodded, but she didn't make any other gesture.

Leslie felt as if she had done something wrong. Maybe Lola thought she put Valgooney up to the kidnapping.

Lola turned to Earl. "I say let her sweat it out a night in here. Serve her right."

"Don't know about that," Earl said.

"Ain't nothin' we can do until Richardson get here."

Earl looked at Leslie. "Guess we goin'. You goin' stay?"

"Yes sir."

Lola stood up. "It was nice to meet you," Leslie said to Lola, who had only nodded, once again, making Leslie feel like it was all her fault. That nod seemed more like a spanking than a real spanking. That was power, she thought.

When they left, Leslie sat down where they had been sitting.

Leslie noticed that every few minutes, two officers who were talking looked over at her, as if they knew her. Probably from being shown on the tube all over America, she thought. Or maybe they were thinking about arresting her too.

Earlier, as she drove to the jail, she turned on the radio to NPR. She caught the news halfway through the broadcast:

"Sources say nine thousand people who attended the march have already filed suits against the federal government for not protecting their civil rights. An attorney involved for some of the plaintiffs said that these lawsuits could avalanche into the largest case ever filed against the United States government. The march was the largest protest ever held for gay rights. Our estimates show at least three million marchers participated. In other news, Valgooney Gore, one of the organizers of the March on Myrtle, is still under arrest in the attempted kidnapping of Rosemary Kennedy. There is still no report on whether there is a connection between the march and the kidnapping."

She sipped on the last of the coffee she had purchased from the vending machine down the hall. She felt wired, a kind of wired she hadn't felt since college when she and Andrea would stay up all night cramming for exams; the kind of wired when you finally knew what love meant, like she had with Andrea; the kind of wired when you knew something had awakened in you. You couldn't sleep; you didn't dare sleep because the magic might end if you did. Her body knew; her mind knew.

She wished she had thought about bringing a book. She didn't even know the last time she read a book.

"You know," Andrea would say every once in a while, "just because we're out of college doesn't mean you stop exercising your brain."

Then, out of guilt, she would go to the bookstore and buy the latest bestseller. She knew Andrea was right, but for once, she wanted to do something that began within— not something that was imposed on her—something she thought about; something beyond the guilt. Hadn't she gotten a business degree out of guilt? Hadn't she gone into real estate out of guilt? Her guilt was obese.

She looked around the sitting room, if that's what they called it. It wasn't a room. It was the next thing to a jail cell. She thought the seat was as uncomfortable as the night she waited to hear anything about Andrea.

Only "family" was allowed in the hospital room. So she sat in the drab gray room, waiting, waiting, waiting, like some second-class citizen who didn't dare darken the door of the woman with whom she had shared the last ten years of her life.

When the nurse went down another corridor, Leslie sneaked into Andrea's room. In the low light, Andrea's face already looked ashen, like death. She stood near the door, not knowing what to do if Andrea was already dead.

"Andrea," she whispered.

Andrea didn't move.

"Andrea," she said, a little louder, but she couldn't move from where she was standing.

Andrea still didn't move.

"Andrea," she said loudly.

Andrea opened her eyes, startled. "Why haven't you come to see me?"

Leslie walked over to the side of the bed and sat as close as she could to her. She held her hand, the one that didn't have the intravenous tubes stuck into it.

"They wouldn't let me."

"What bullshit," Andrea whispered.

"I'm scared."

"You are? How do you think I feel?" Andrea laughed, weakly.

"It's not funny, asshole."

"Calling your lover an 'asshole' at a time like this? You'd think I would have gotten involved with a classier chick," she whispered.

Leslie kissed her hand.

"I want to tell you something," Andrea said, still weakly whispering. "Loving you was the best thing I ever did with my life."

Leslie wiped her eyes with the sleeve of her shirt as she looked around the police department, as she waited to see if Valgooney was going to get out on bail. No one had ever said that to her, not before, not since. No one had loved her like that—unconditionally—not even her mother.

Valgooney sat in a chair in the holding cell with three other women. One woman, who looked like a prostitute, was talking to another woman in low whispers. Every once in a while, they would laugh. Another woman sat in the chair closest to Valgooney. She tried not to catch her eye, so instead she looked at the woman's black leather boots that had silver toes. But the woman spoke to her anyway.

"Sure do need a smoke break, know what I mean?"

Valgooney nodded.

The woman scooted her chair closer to Valgooney. "If you don't mind me asking, what's a knockout like you done to get locked up?"

"I tried to kidnap a vegetable."

"You mean steal it?"

"Something like that."

"Now ain't that something. Arresting a good-looking woman for stealing a damn vegetable. What's the world coming to? I tell ya." She held out her hand. "My name's Samantha, but my friends call me 'Squirrel.'"

Valgooney shook her hand.

Squirrel looked around the cell. "Know what I did?"

Not waiting for Valgooney to answer, Squirrel continued.

"Heard about the march?"

Valgooney nodded.

"This Reverend Farnsworth and his congregation had this hose goin' full blast. They was tryin' to wash everybody's sin away, I guess. When they done hit these here leather boots and put my cigarette out, weren't but one thing to do. Smacked the shit out of him. That's what I done. May have broke his jaw. Ain't sure he's goin' preach for a while."

"Bravo." Valgooney said.

"Like that, huh?"

"Sometimes, some people need a shut-up smack."

"Yeah, boy." Squirrel leaned back in her chair and stretched out her legs. The silver toes pointed up.

Valgooney watched Squirrel take a long look at the prostitute, whose cleavage was bulging out of her blouse.

At seven a.m. an officer rushed past Leslie, who had finally closed her eyes, nodding off to sleep. All through the night, when her head rolled back too hard, she would wake up.

Three other officers ran in the same direction: toward the front door. She heard the door slam. Even the officer behind the window looked interested.

"They're out there, all right!" she heard the woman say to another officer across the room.

Leslie wondered who, but she didn't want to ask. She walked over to a small window near the front.

In the early morning light, she saw hundreds of people with signs walking in circles around the front lawn. The officers who had run out of the building were standing in a row across the front steps with their arms crossed.

And a chant began.

"FREE VALGOONEY. FREE VALGOONEY. FREE VALGOONEY."

"You're with her, aren't you?"

Leslie turned around. It was the female officer from the counter.

"Did she do it?"

"I haven't a clue." Leslie turned to look out the window.

The officer moved close to the window beside her.

"Nothing like this has ever happened here before. Will you look at all of those people? Your friend sure can start some trouble. She's already been arrested before. Why, they might just throw the book at her this time."

One officer turned to the other officer and said, "You remember the trouble she started with the post office, don't you?"

The woman nodded. "She sure picks some doozeys to get involved with."

As they watched, a black limousine pulled up the circular drive. The chauffeur got out and opened the door. A tall, beefy white man in a black business suit with a Carolina blue tie got out of the limo. The chauffeur slammed the door shut.

The front door opened and one of the officers who had been observing the crowd escorted the man into the foyer.

"This is Ms. Gore's attorney," the officer said to the female officer still standing beside Leslie.

Leslie, Valgooney, and Bill Richardson walked out the front door and toward the limousine. When someone in the crowd recognized Valgooney, the crowd began chanting: "VAL-GOON-EY, VAL-GOON-EY."

She waved as the chauffeur gently pushed her into the back seat as the crowd gathered close to the limo.

He closed the door and walked around to the front. As soon as he was in the driver's seat, he asked, "Where to now?"

"Let's drop these ladies off first, then it's back to the airport. Val, you'll have to tell him where you want to go."

"When you get to Main, take a left on Nixon and then left on 63rd."

The driver nodded.

She turned to Leslie. "It's low tide. Want to walk over to the island?"

"Okay."

"What time does your plane leave?" Valgooney asked Richardson.

"Anytime I'm ready. It's a charter, the company plane."

"That's convenient."

"Especially when there's a damsel in distress, although you girls look like you can take care of yourselves." He laughed.

Leslie thought his laugh sounded full, like a stuffed turkey would sound if it could laugh and talk.

The driver turned onto Nixon and then 63rd. When the street ended near the channel, he stopped the car.

Valgooney wrapped her arms around Richardson's neck and hugged him. "Thank you again."

"Stay out of trouble, will you? And don't forget to fulfill your community service." He shook one of his thick fingers at her.

"I won't."

The driver opened the door, and Leslie and Valgooney got out.

They waited until the car had turned around and was driving away before they waved and began to walk down the sidewalk to where it dead-ended into the sand. They walked past Leslie's mother's house.

"That's where my mother lives."

Valgooney looked at the house and then at Leslie. "Beautiful house. So is your mother."

"You know my mother?"

"We have not been officially introduced, but we have nodded at each other over the last several years."

"My mother didn't tell me…" but Leslie didn't finish the sentence.

"Tell you what?"

"That she had come in close proximity to you."

"Well, we have."

"Oh, I believe you." Leslie looked down at the sand they were now walking on. "Mother," she said. "My mother is such a mother."

Valgooney laughed. "Aren't all mothers? That's what makes them so wonderful."

As they continued to walk along the sand in low tide, there were a few people fishing and lying in the sun.

"By the way, what did Richardson mean by 'community service'?" Leslie asked.

"He worked out an arrangement for me to do 3,000 hours of community service, if the magistrate would drop all of the charges."

"Three thousand?"

"Guess I'm lucky that Richardson used to party with Ted Kennedy. But he said that I can never say why I tried to kidnap Rosemary. That was part of the stipulation."

As they began to cross the channel with the ocean to their right, it looked like they were walking on water. It made Leslie wonder if that's what Jesus' disciples had really seen. Leslie felt the ripples of the dried, packed sand under her shoes.

"You can hide out on the island for a while."

Leslie cocked her head to the side to look at Valgooney. "You mean for the rest of the day?"

"For as long as you want. I figure you'll need to let things die down for a while."

"That's an understatement," Leslie said, and then shook her head.

"I'm guessing that after losing your huge commission, it might be fun to stay in real style—a trailer—as a break."

Leslie laughed. "I could wave at my mother from across the channel."

"You know the media is probably at your hotel or peeking in your windows in Charlotte. So stay a while."

"I might take you up on that." Leslie smiled. "If you'll take me on your next freeing-the-crabs escapade."

Julie E. Townsend

"If I get caught for one more thing, I may have to serve some actual time, get stuck in jail cells with women that have nicknames like 'Squirrel.'"

Leslie whipped her head around. She felt her neck crack when she did so. "Squirrel?"

"Squirrel," Valgooney repeated.

It had to be the same woman, Leslie thought. "If I can't go on one of your seafood missions, then maybe I'll join one of those groups for 'those who have been abused in the name of Jesus.'" She chuckled. "You know what you are, don't you? You're some kind of anti-establishment Jesus."

"I'm not anti-anything except *anti-mean* to animals and humans. I prefer "Seafood Jesus," she said.

Leslie smiled at those words, and then she turned around to look across the channel at her mother's house. She closed her eyes and visualized her favorite Andrea look: those long eyelashes hanging over her eyes. For a moment, a minuscule moment, she didn't feel any pain.

They walked for a few minutes longer without saying anything, avoiding the puddles of water that the high tide left behind for the low tide.

"Know what the attendant said about Rosemary?" Valgooney asked. "When he told her why he had to borrow her? She smiled. He said that no one had seen her smile, ever, except in old family pictures."

EPILOGUE

Father: I do have, have another question.... What bothered you, you the most about me? My relationship; my dyslexia; my weight-gain; or your hopes, hopes? You know that I always send you thoughts, wherever you might be now, now.... I always did, did since childhood and have before 1941, and I have until now, now. You know that I heard, heard about your stroke so many years ago, ago, and wondered if you knew, knew, what I feel like? It's difficult to forgive someone of robbing, robbing you of your life. Sometimes, I try to remember what I learned from one of the nuns, nuns: "You must forgive, but that's different from forgetting." I'm trying, trying to get there. I have spent a lifetime, here, inside of me, trying to get there, inside these echoes of the impasse between, between love and hate. So I'll try, try to forgive you for stopping me from a relationship with *her*, but you never stopped me from loving *her.*

Julie E. Townsend